FLASH OF FIRE

Dogleg Island Mystery #6

Donna Ball

Blue Merle Publishing

First published September 2023 by Blue Merle Publishing
www.bluemerlepublishers.com

Print ISBN:978-1-7351271-9-4

Cover art by www.bigstock.com

CONTENTS

A NOTE TO READERS

Flash of Fire takes place in the summer after the events of *Flash in the Dark* and before the Christmas events of *The Good Shepherd*. Readers will enjoy reading these stories in order.

CHAPTER ONE

They were eighteen miles outside of Tallahassee when Ziggy shot that woman. Ziggy—so named because, with his waist-length beard, dark shades, and stocking cap, he was a dead ringer for that guy Billy Gibbons from the band ZZ Top—had always been a loose cannon. Why in the hell he was allowed to carry a weapon was something the rest of them would be debating as long as they were free to do so. Which, in retrospect, wouldn't be that long.

Rocketman, the de facto leader of the group since Dean had driven a stolen car filled with explosives off a bridge last year, blamed himself—although not as much as he blamed that asshead, Ziggy. Rocketman had already decided this would be his last job. Even though he hadn't told the others yet, he had seen the writing on the wall since the bank job outside of Memphis. They'd almost gotten caught with that one. If it hadn't been for the incompetence of the security guard, who'd shot at Cappy's head and blew out the bank window instead, they'd all be facing prison time by now—except Cappy, of course, who'd be dead.

There were four of them left now, and no one knew anyone else's real name—not even Tulip and Cappy, who spent half their time screwing each other with the ferocity of a couple of mad rabbits and the other half so high they probably couldn't have remembered their real names if they'd been forced to do so at gunpoint. The idea of anonymity had been Dean's, who had been called Dean because of the way he held their ragtag little band together like the headmaster at a school for wayward kids. The logic was if the Feds ever caught up with them nobody would be able to give them any information they didn't have— including the real identities of the other members of the group. Dean was always thinking of things like that, which was how they had remained in business as long as they had. Of course, that had all been back in the beginning when they believed in themselves and their mission with a passion only twenty- year-olds can fully possess. When they not only believed they could save the planet, but that it was a place worth saving.

After the cops chased Dean over that bridge, somebody said something about "one last job in Dean's honor," and it had made a bleak kind of sense at the time. They planted a bomb in a warehouse filled with planet-killing pesticide just to see it burn and, because Dean had taught them well, they got away with it. But it cost money to stay on the run, so they blew a safe at a check-cashing joint and that place, too, burned to the ground. After that, it became more about staying alive than saving the world, but they kept going because they had no alternative. But it wasn't until after the bank job that Rocketman really knew it was over, for him at least.

Anybody could see they'd lost their passion for the work, even Ziggy, who'd more or less been the standard bearer for the cause since Dean died. Nonetheless, Ziggy managed to rally them into action one more time. One last job. That was what he kept saying as he laid out the particulars of the bombing that would be the pinnacle of their careers. One last, dramatic statement, and they'd all go down in a blaze of glory. Except Rocketman had no intention of going down at all. How many movies had started out with the career criminal ready to call it quits and haul ass for Mexico just as soon as he pulled "one last job"? And not a single one of those movies had ended well for the guy who didn't know enough to quit while he was ahead.

They'd had a good run. But it was like the dude said, You gotta know when to fold 'em.

They stopped at an all-night gas station on the edge of some little nowhere town outside of Tallahassee to fuel up. It was 4:30 in the morning and they were the only customers. The clerk, a pudgy woman with an acne-scarred face and ill-fitting jeans, was leaning against the phone booth just outside the door when they drove up, smoking a cigarette and watching them through narrowed eyes. Rocketman couldn't blame her; they were a rough looking crew even when they hadn't been driving all night.

Rocketman, Ziggy, and Cappy got out. Tulip stayed in the back, filing her nails and munching on the last dregs of a bag of Fritos. The clerk, still watching them suspiciously, tossed her cigarette onto the pavement and turned to go inside. Cappy called after her, "Hey! Five dollars on the pump!"

She went inside to turn on the pump, still keeping a wary eye on them, and Ziggy and Rocketman followed her in. Cappy pumped the gas while Ziggy wandered around, picking out more snacks. Rocketman browsed a small collection of magazines in the back aisle and picked up one called *Florida's Forgotten Treasures*. It had a picture of a blue-green ocean and a white sand beach on the front, and inside were features on the hidden islands of the Gulf Coast... tiny barrier islands with names like Captiva, Wild Horse, Dogleg, Venice, where pirates had buried treasure and blockade runners had hidden their ships during the Civil War. Some of them were only reachable by ferry, and most only had a token law enforcement presence. Imagine, paradise right here in the American South. It looked too good to be true, but there it was in all the blues and greens and fabulous red sunsets of the ocean. Fishing villages, sandy roads winding through the dunes, cedar shacks. A fellow could get lost in a place like that with no trouble at all.

Ziggy had reached the counter, and Rocketman started to put the magazine back on the shelf. He heard the clerk say, "Hey, don't I know you from somewhere?" Ziggy mumbled something in the negative and out of the corner of his eye Rocketman saw Ziggy reach for his wallet. The clerk insisted, "Wait a minute! I know. You're that guy in the magazines. You're..."

The next thing Rocketman heard was the explosion of a gunshot, and when he spun around the clerk was no longer there. A red puddle crept from behind the counter and across the linoleum floor.

Rocketman launched himself across the room, grabbing Ziggy's arm, shouting, "What'd you do that for? Are you crazy? What the fuck, man, what the..."

Ziggy flung him away, sweating, red-faced, his eyes wild. The gun in his hand still smelled like cordite. "She recognized me!" he shouted back. "She was gonna call the cops! What was I supposed to do, you stupid shit?"

Rocketman stared at him, incredulity and outrage spreading through him faster than the blood was traveling across the floor. "She didn't recognize you, asshead," he managed after what seemed like a long moment. "She thought you were fucking Billy Gibbons!"

Rocketman didn't wait to see whether the truth registered in Ziggy's eyes, or if he'd even heard him. He swept his own gaze around the small space, hot with fury and cold with panic. Somebody could come along at any minute. They'd left fingerprints everywhere. Of all the crazy, stupid, *reckless*...

One last job. It was always that one last job.

He saw a display of kerosene cans beside the window and grabbed one, twisting off the top. He tossed the contents across the counter, trying not to look at the body with its face blown off, then over the shelves. After a moment Ziggy, who might be stupid but wasn't completely worthless, got another can and started to empty it across the back shelves. The whole process took less than thirty seconds. They threw the empty cans on the floor and Ziggy tossed a match as they ran out the door.

Cappy and Tulip were waiting in the car, looking alarmed and excited. "What happened?" Cappy demanded. "What's going on?"

While Tulip said, "Was that a gun? It sounded like a gun."

Rocketman got in the driver's seat as the flames from the building turned the night to orange, and he slammed the door without answering. He didn't even wait for Ziggy to close his door before he took off.

They called him Rocketman, not only because he was a genius with homemade bombs, but because he drove like a bat out of hell, and that was what he did then. Dean once said Rocketman could have raced with NASCAR if he'd wanted to. This was not the first time Rocketman wished he'd made a different career choice.

Miles swept by on the flat, empty Florida backroads while Rocketman pounded his fist against the steering wheel, shouted obscenities at Ziggy, threatened to end him in every torturous way possible, and cursed the day Ziggy's mother had ever opened her legs for his father. At one point Ziggy launched himself across the seat at Rocketman, grabbing for his throat, and Rocketman almost rolled the car. Cappy, who was skinny but mean, broke it up, and after that, the dark miles passed in silence.

It was hours later that Rocketman realized he still had that magazine about the Florida coast, stuffed between his seat and the console. Not long after that, he saw a road sign that read, "Dogleg Island, 60 miles." It seemed like an omen, somehow, and his shoulders relaxed. He actually smiled.

One last job. Oh, hell, yeah. And he knew exactly what that job would be.

CHAPTER TWO

The best thing about being alive—in Flash's view, anyway—was that there was always something new every day. Most of the time, those things were good, but even when they weren't... well, you just never knew. Things could still turn out for the good.

Take today, for instance. This was the day Flash and Aggie were moving from their old police station in the tiny room next to the hair salon to the big suite in the old Grady warehouse on the water. Flash thought it was a grand idea. There was a glass door with Aggie's name in gold lettering on it, a maritime museum on the top floor, and a view of the waterfront sidewalk from Aggie's office, where Flash could imagine spending many a pleasant hour watching people walk by. The whole place smelled like fresh paint and things waiting to be discovered. But even though Aggie had been the one who thought of moving the police station in the first place, and even though she had spent practically the whole summer supervising every board that was laid and every nail that was driven, the closer moving day grew, the more worried she became. She thought it was going to turn out bad. Flash knew better.

Like most border collies, Flash had an innate sense of order, which meant that he could immediately recognize whether there had been sixteen watches in the jewelry store window yesterday, and today there were only fifteen. He knew when twenty children had boarded the school bus and only nineteen had gotten off, which had come in handy once when Nathan Ferguson had been discovered sleeping in the back of the bus. He also had an eye for detail, which Aggie said was important in police work, and a keen understanding of the English language—which, when it came right down to it, was all a fellow really needed when his main job was listening. Everything Flash had ever learned about police work came from listening to Aggie, and most everything else he knew came from listening to other people. That was how he knew today was going to be a great day.

"I don't know," Aggie said now, pulling up a stool to the breakfast bar. Her brow was furrowed with anxiety. "Maybe moving was a mistake. The police station should be downtown, in the center of things, where people can find us. It's always been downtown. Maybe people won't like us being all the way over on the waterfront."

Grady was at the stove, stirring up scrambled eggs. The fragrance of fried bacon and toasting bread filled the air. Ryan Grady was Flash's second favorite person in the world, next to Aggie, and not just because he made an amazing breakfast. Grady, who was already dressed this morning in his green Murphy County Sheriff's Deputy uniform, was in charge of keeping the bad guys under control in Ocean City, on the other side of the bridge. Aggie and Flash were in charge of the bad guys on Dogleg Island if they happened to make it that far. So far—with one or two notable exceptions—Grady had done such a good job on his side of the bridge that Flash's job wasn't even very hard. There was also, of course, the fact that Grady had been married to Aggie almost as long as Flash could remember, and had loved her even longer than that, which was enough to make him Number One in Flash's book—or Number Two, as it happened.

Grady turned with the pan of scrambled eggs in his hand but hesitated over her plate. "How's the morning sickness?"

Aggie held up her thumb and forefinger in a circle, indicating Okay. "Your mom's tip about saltines and flat ginger ale before I get out of bed worked great," she said. "And I'm starved."

"Good deal." Grady dished out a portion of scrambled eggs onto her plate and divided what remained in the pan between his plate and Flash's bowl.

"It takes almost forty-five seconds longer to get to Island Road from there," Aggie pointed out, picking up her fork.

"From where?"

"The new police station."

He shrugged. "Yeah, but it takes thirty seconds less to get to Beachside Park." Grady slathered two pieces of toast with butter and jam and put them on her plate, pointing with his knife. "Eat that," he told her. "You need to gain two pounds before your next OB appointment."

Aggie tried not to roll her eyes. "Said no woman ever." Nonetheless, she piled eggs onto a slice of toast and bit into it. "We should have had a ribbon cutting like everyone wanted to."

"You're the one who said it was too much."

"I know." She took another bite of toast. "But what if I was wrong?"

"Baby, you're never wrong."

Flash, sitting at Aggie's side, waited patiently while Grady cut a slice of toast into four squares, just the way Flash liked it, placed the toast in his bowl, and topped it with two slices of bacon. He put the bowl on the floor. "Chow down, big guy," he said.

Flash wasted no time doing as he was told.

"The thing is," Aggie went on, "it might have been a good thing to have a little ceremony there like Lorraine wanted to. You know, to kind of celebrate a new beginning. It might help people forget. That's what Lorraine said, anyway. The newspaper could take pictures, we'd have cupcakes, and Pete could make a speech. He's head of the council, and he's good at speeches. The paper always quotes him."

Grady dished out bacon onto her plate. "Well, it's too late now."

She sighed and picked up a slice of bacon with her fingers. "I guess." She bit into the bacon. "It just seems like a shame."

Grady said, "Speaking of Beachside Park..."

She lifted an eyebrow. "Were we?"

"What was that bunch of ragged-looking refugees from a hippie commune doing out there yesterday marching around in circles with signs?"

"Exercising their right to peaceful assembly," Aggie replied. "Perhaps you've heard of it?"

He poured a glass of milk and set it in front of her plate. "What are they assembling against?"

She shrugged. "I'm not entirely sure. Something about the new environmental center that's opening in Mercury Park this week."

"Well, that's a new one." He took two more slices of toast from the toaster and began to make a sandwich with the bacon and eggs on his plate. "Protestors demonstrating *against* protecting the environment."

"I don't think they see it that way."

He gave a mild snort of derision. "They never do. You know, there wasn't a single local face in the crowd. What the hell do a bunch of outsiders care about what happens on Dogleg, anyway?"

"We live in a global community, Ryan," she said. She looked at him curiously. "What were you doing at the park yesterday?"

"Well," he admitted, wrapping the egg sandwich in a paper towel, "I was supposed to meet my girlfriend there yesterday afternoon, but she never showed, so I decided to hang around and score a little coke."

"Cute." Aggie scooped up a forkful of eggs. "You know the one thing I hope the baby doesn't inherit from you, Ryan?"

"If I had to guess…" He pretended thoughtfulness. "My sense of humor?"

She cocked a finger at him. "You'd guess right."

He filled a thermos with coffee. "Drink your milk," he ordered, "take your vitamins and don't walk to work. The heat index is going to be 102 today. Take care of my little football star."

Aggie took her glass of milk to the refrigerator, removed a carton of ice cream from the freezer, and added a scoop to her milk. "Ry, I have to tell you something."

He looked at her cautiously, thermos and sandwich in hand. "What?"

Aggie returned to the breakfast bar with her improvised milkshake and sat down. "It's a girl."

Flash looked up from licking his bowl clean, matching the curious look on Grady's face.

"How do you know?" Grady said. "We haven't even gotten a sonogram yet."

She explained patiently, "I'm growing a human inside me. I think I'd be the first to know the gender. It's a girl and her name is Lillian Lorraine Grady."

Grady smiled and reached across the counter to caress her cheek. "Yeah, it is," he said.

Then he stretched over the bar to kiss Aggie's lips. "I gotta run, babe. The sheriff called an early meeting and I'm late. I love you."

Surprised disappointment flooded her face. "But

I thought you were going to come with me to the office this morning. You said you wanted to see how everything turned out, and with it being our first day in the new place and all. . ." Her voice trailed off.

He looked for a moment as though he didn't remember ever having had such a conversation, but covered it quickly with, "Maybe this weekend. Have a good first day. Send me a picture." He grabbed his phone and keys from the bowl on the counter and headed toward the door.

Aggie made a brief, sour face, then turned on her stool to call after him, "Don't speed across the bridge! I am not raising this baby by myself!"

He blew a kiss at her and pulled the door closed behind him.

Aggie added, because she never let him start a shift without saying it, "I love you!"

He waved his hand in acknowledgment as he passed the kitchen window, heading for his truck.

Aggie shrugged off her disappointment with a sigh. "I guess we're the only ones who think reopening the building is a big deal, huh, Flash?"

In response, Flash raced to the door, opened it with two paws, and dashed outside to wait by the Dogleg Island police car that was parked in the driveway. Aggie grinned as she got up to take her dishes to the dishwasher. "Husbands come and go," she called after him, "but a good dog will never let you down."

Flash pretended not to hear, but she saw him grinning through the kitchen window.

CHAPTER THREE

Flash, a black and white border collie with blue eyes—a rarity in border collies, he had been told—had been helping Aggie keep the peace on Dogleg Island for almost four years now. His main job was keeping watch over things which, on an island with a population of 422, wasn't that hard until the tourists came. During the hot, bright, coconut-oil-smelling summers, so many strangers came to town that it was all he and Aggie could do to keep up with them, and hardly any of them knew the rules. No crossing against the light. No skateboarding in the street. No fighting in public. No taking things from shops without paying for them. It was Flash's job to notice when people broke the rules, and Aggie's job to write the tickets. There was always plenty of work to do in the summer.

It was September now, still hot and bright, and while most of the tourists had gone home, the people with summer houses and weekend houses were still here. That meant there was plenty of policing to do. Aggie often complained that the census-takers weren't doing them any favor counting only full-time residents among the population of Dogleg, since the actual number was easily twice, if not three times that amount. Still, September was the beginning of the down season for Dogleg. The ice cream shop was still open, and the tee shirt shop still sold key chains and souvenir mugs to visitors, but the streets were a lot quieter now. Aggie and Flash were no longer up at dawn patrolling the streets or riding out after dark to tell people to turn the music down. It was the perfect time for them to move into their new headquarters.

The completion of the final renovation of the old Grady warehouse building was, in truth, a very big deal—for everyone except, apparently, Ryan Grady himself. Eight months ago, a battle had been fought in that building; blood had stained the weathered brick floors and bullet holes peppered the walls. Lives had been shattered. Most of the people who had been there that night—which included virtually everyone on the island—would have been happy to see it torn down, for they would never look at the stately edifice again without reliving the horror of those hours.

For a long time, Aggie had been one of those people who wouldn't mind seeing the building demolished. But once she had made the decision to stay and fight for the life she and Ryan had built here, she knew that erasing all evidence of the trauma they had all endured together would not heal their wounds, but only hide them. The warehouse had been a landmark on Dogleg Island for over 150 years. It had endured hurricanes, floods, and cannon fire. It had welcomed cargo ships in the days when the Grady family had transported barrels of turpentine to the other forty-eight states and had stored foodstuffs and household necessities for the island in times of war. One awful night did not define the building any more than it defined the lives of everyone who had been there.

Since the Grady family had donated the property to the community in the 1960s, the warehouse had been used mostly for meetings and civic events. There were a few administrative offices downstairs, and a maritime museum upstairs. Very little had been done to update the building in sixty years beyond the addition of public restrooms and a small kitchen for catering events. When Aggie had first begun to investigate the idea of moving the police station from its one-room location in the downtown shopping district to an unused suite of rooms in the warehouse, the response had been lukewarm. However, when, weeks after the event that the papers loved to call the War of Dogleg Island, she came back with a new determination and a new proposal, she was astonished by the vigor with which it was received.

Margaret Dillon, the island administrator who had never been a big fan of Aggie's, unearthed a grant that would not only pay for the new police station but would also cover updates to the existing administrative offices, including—everyone was delighted to learn—a new central heating and air-conditioning system. Ryan's dad, Salty, had worked with local contractors to draw up plans for the renovations. Local businesses donated supplies —paint, flooring, windows, even furniture—and the island council, led by Ryan's brother Pete, had agreed to allocate funds for the rest. Pete's wife, Lorraine, had inspired the garden club to take on the project of relandscaping the ragged lawn on the backside of the property into an attractive park with flower beds, picnic tables, and even a community garden. The benches along the waterfront walkway had been spruced up with new green paint, and cement planters filled with succulents lined the promenade. Ryan and Pete, along with most of the other men on the island, had spent their free time swinging hammers and painting trim. It was as though everyone who had lived through the War of Dogleg Island was determined to exorcise the demons from that place, and the project had become a real community event.

At 7:55 a. m. , Aggie pulled into the parking space behind the building marked "Reserved: Chief of Police." There were two other spots next to hers with "police" stenciled on the yellow curbs. Mo's vehicle was in one of them. The other one was empty. Aggie tried not to look at the empty spot.

Aggie and Flash got out and spent a moment admiring the building's newly sandblasted, pink-brick exterior. The surrounding landscaping was mostly crushed shell paths and pine bark accented by hardy succulents, thanks to the advice of Mason McMasters, a local landscaper who had volunteered his time and donated most of the materials for the project. The few raised flower beds Lorraine had insisted upon were drooping badly after a month-long drought. Aggie saw Father Dave, in a floppy straw hat, torn denim shorts, and a faded Tulane tee shirt, working one of the plots in the community garden at the far end of the lot, and she waved to him. He raised his arm in return and then went back to work pulling up dead, end-of-season plants.

"You know, Flash," Aggie remarked, still gazing at the building, "it wouldn't have been a terrible idea to have Father Dave do a blessing or something. If there even is such a thing as a blessing for a police station."

Flash gave her an impatient look and raced up the sidewalk to the door. Aggie followed more slowly, trying to appreciate the moment.

There were two entrances to the police station. The one that opened onto the parking lot was blackout hurricane glass framed in steel, and it had "Dogleg Island Police Department" painted on it in gold lettering. The other door opened into the hallway of the main building that led to the administrative offices. When Aggie reached the outside door where Flash was waiting, she found it locked, which wasn't particularly surprising since it wasn't quite 8:00 a. m. and office hours—also clearly lettered on the door —were 8:00 to 5:00. What was surprising was that Aggie's key was not on her key ring. She remembered placing it in the bowl on the counter with the intention of putting it on her key ring, but obviously, she hadn't gotten around to it. She made a sound of frustration and embarrassment and turned to walk around to the front entrance. "Typical Monday," she muttered.

Flash, not in the least inconvenienced, dashed around the building ahead of her. But, as excited as he was about their first day in the new place, when Aggie opened the big wooden doors and stepped inside, he did not run ahead. Aggie paused, looking around the vast open space that was so charged with memories and, out of respect to her, Flash paused too.

Due to her pregnancy, Aggie had not been allowed inside the building while the final painting and varnishing of the floors had been completed, so it had been almost two weeks since she and Flash had been here. A lot had changed. Light flooded in from the row of new windows overhead, but when Flash looked at them, he heard the sound of screams and gunfire and breaking glass. The brick walls had been painted a nice off-white, but Flash could still see the bullet scars. The old floors had been sanded and refinished to a bright oak sheen and the whole place smelled like fresh paint and varnish, but beneath it, Flash could still smell the blood. He did not have to look at Aggie to know she smelled it too.

But only for a moment. Aggie took a breath, forced a smile, and dropped her hand to Flash's head. "It looks great, doesn't it, Flash? Just like brand new."

Flash smiled his gratitude to her, shook the taint of the past off his coat, and trotted toward the wide hallway beside the stairs. There was a signboard there with white letters that listed the offices that could be found down that hallway: Police Station, Island

Records, Administrator, Meeting Rooms. But of much more importance was what was displayed next to the sign. Flash sat down when he saw it. Aggie, coming to stand beside him, caught her breath.

An alcove had been cut into the wall. Inside the alcove was a shelf holding a bronzed Dogleg Island police cap and a badge. The plaque below it read, *In loving memory of Officer Samuel Robinson Brown, who gave his life in defense of the citizens of Dogleg Island, February 14, 2023. "No greater love has any man than this, that he would lay down his life for a friend." –John 15:13.*

Aggie stood there for a moment, swallowing hard, and then she brought her fingers to the brim of her cap in a salute. She turned and walked with Flash down the hall toward their new home.

CHAPTER FOUR

A ggie could see the lights were on behind the frosted glass door of the hallway entrance to the police station, and when she opened the door Flash wriggled through in front of her. Aggie stepped inside and was greeted by a chorus of "Surprise!" The room was filled with people: Pete and Lorraine, Sheriff Bishop, Margaret Dillon, every single member of the island council; her second-in-command, Mo, her office manager, Sally Ann, and, of course, her husband. Most of the business owners were there, too—Jason and Bret from the Island Bistro, Tom from Saylor's Surf Shop, Mrs. Mosley the baker, Ken Lindley from The Beach Shack, Trish from the beauty salon, and half a dozen more. Jess Krieger, publisher and editor of the Dogleg Island weekly newspaper, snapped photos. There was a balloon banner over the door and a sheet cake with the police department logo on it displayed on the reception counter. Everyone was laughing and raising their glasses to her, and Flash stood at the front of the crowd, wagging his tail as proudly as though he had arranged the whole thing himself.

Aggie stood there for a moment with her hands pressed to her cheeks in astonishment. "How did you... when... who...?"

Lorraine pulled her forward, pressing a plastic cup of something sparkling into her hand. "You were outvoted," she informed her. "Of course we're having a dedication party! As hard as everybody's worked all year and as much as you've looked forward to your new office? That's sparkling cider, by the way," she said, indicating the contents of Aggie's cup. "Hold on to it, there's going to be a toast. *And* a ribbon cutting," she added pertly. "That's why Ryan took your key— so we could put the ribbon across the door while you went around to the front entrance."

Aggie laughed when she saw her husband sitting on the corner of Sally Ann's desk, grinning and dangling a key between his fingers. "I don't know what to say," she began, and before she could think of anything, Jerome Bishop put his arm around her shoulders in a firm hug.

"Congratulations, sweetheart," he said. "You got it done." He added with a wink, "How's little Jerome doing?"

The sheriff was a big man with a deep, resonant voice that radiated both authority and compassion, which was, Aggie had always thought, one of the reasons he had stayed in office for so long. When this building was under siege eight months ago, it was his voice that had cut across the chaos and calmed the terrified crowd. *This is Sheriff Bishop. Stay where you are. We are coming for you.*

Aggie pushed aside the memory and smiled. "It's a girl," Aggie informed him.

Bishop replied equitably, "Well, you should know."

Jess Krieger said, "How about a quote for the paper, Chief?"

Aggie replied, "The Dogleg Island Police Department is honored to be a part of this new chapter in the island's history."

He jotted it down. "I can always count on you, Aggie. How about a picture of you and Ms. Dillon cutting the cake?"

Bishop said, "I'll let you get back to your fans, Aggie. But I'd like a word with you before I leave, if you have time."

"Sure thing," Aggie said.

Margaret Dillon, in a crisp navy suit and white blouse, came forward and put her arm through Aggie's. "Of course," she told Jess smoothly, "it was a group effort. We couldn't have managed any of it without the cooperation of the whole town. And be sure to add that we'll be having a grand opening for the public in a few weeks. No date as yet, but we'll let you know."

She led Aggie toward the desk where the cake was displayed. "We need to talk," she added in a lower voice.

Aggie lifted an eyebrow, but before she could inquire, Jess began lining everybody up for the shot —Aggie and Margaret, each with a hand on the cake knife, Mo and Sally Ann on either side, and the entire Island Council standing behind. Flash made his own place directly in front of the desk. The photograph was taken, the cake was served, and the room filled with chatter. Sally Ann, in red-and-white checked glasses, pigtails, and a flowered maxi-skirt, took over cake-serving duty, reminding Aggie with her usual Sally-Ann-like efficiency, "Don't forget we have time set aside to talk today. It's on your calendar."

"Yay." Aggie smiled weakly. She knew exactly what Sally Ann wanted to talk about, and she was not looking forward to it. "My first interview in my new office."

"Also," Sally Ann said, handing a square of cake on a paper plate to Pete, "Mo needs a minute when you've got it."

Aggie sighed. "Right. Of course she does." This day was already getting out of control.

Pete said to Aggie, "How's our little quarterback coming along?"

"Aggie says it's a girl," Grady supplied, coming up behind his wife.

"Well, Aggie should know," conceded Pete. "And who says girls can't be quarterbacks?"

Aggie grinned. "I knew there was a reason I liked you, Pete." She took a bite of her cake and gestured around the room with her fork. "How'd you guys pull this off, anyway?"

Pete's eyes traveled with wry affection across the room to his wife, Lorraine, who was proudly showing off the artwork—on loan from the library in Panama

City—to Brett and Jason. "How do you think?"

Grady took his piece of cake and the three of them moved away from the serving station. "No offense babe," he said with a wink, "but you're really slipping if you didn't see this one coming. Maybe you need to go back for a refresher course in basic detection."

"Pregnancy brain," she replied placidly. "And, by the way, that's going to be my excuse for everything for the next six months, just in case you're planning to pull another fast one." Her expression softened as she added to both men, "The memorial turned out really nice, didn't it? Thank you."

Pete said, "That's another reason we wanted you to come through the front door, so you could see the completed display. The plaque almost didn't get here in time."

"Here's your key back." Grady handed it to her. He took another quick bite of cake. "I can't stay long. Somebody's got to run the sheriff's office while the rest of you are out here having fun."

"Well, I hope you'll at least stay for the dedication prayer," said Father Dave, coming to join him. "I've been working on it all week."

He had changed into his black tunic and clerical collar, but still wore the denim shorts and sneakers beneath. On another cleric the outfit might have looked blasphemous, or at least absurd, but the young priest had won the hearts of the islanders over the past couple of years with his laid-back style and ecumenical approach to the ministry, and no one in this room would think of rebuking him.

Aggie said, "So you were in on this too, Father?"

"I was the lookout," he informed her with a wink. "I'm the one who texted Lorraine when you pulled up."

Flash, having greeted everyone in the room and enjoyed more than one piece of cake, trotted up while Aggie was laughing with Father Dave. He had checked out the new file cubby and Officer Mo's private cubicle, which already had a jade plant on the desk and a drawer full of candy. He'd inspected Sally Ann's tall, horseshoe-shaped reception desk and the flags at each entrance. He'd toured their new private office—the one with Aggie's name stenciled in gold on the frosted glass door—and admired the red plaid dog bed in the corner and the oil painting of Flash himself that hung over Aggie's desk. Everything had turned out even better than expected, and Flash thought they were going to be very happy here.

Aggie dropped to one knee beside him and offered him the last bite of her cake on a paper plate. He obligingly scooped it up even though, if truth be told, he was a little tired of the taste of cake. "Now, you see, Flash," Aggie said, draping an arm around his neck. "This only goes to show that sometimes things you think aren't going to work out at all can still turn out good."

Flash grinned at her. His thoughts exactly.

Pete rapped the edge of the cake knife against a coffee mug and called, "Everybody? Everybody, can I have your attention, please?"

The chatter in the room gradually quieted down,

and Aggie stood up. Flash settled down at Aggie's feet, sensing a speech coming on. Pete gave amazing speeches, although sometimes they could run a little long.

"I know we've all got to get to work," Pete said, "so I won't take too much of your time. On behalf of the council, Ms. Dillon, and Chief Malone, I want to thank you for coming out. Particular thanks to my lovely wife, Lorraine Grady..." He raised his cup to Lorraine across the room, who responded by spreading the folds of her colorful palazzo pants into a deep curtsey. "For putting this whole thing together this morning." Everybody applauded. "Mrs. Mosley of Mosley's Sweet Treats for the outstanding refreshments..." More applause and cheers, and the plump-faced Mrs. Mosley blushed and made shooing motions with her hands. "And to Sally Ann Mitchell and Officer Mo Wilson for the decorations." Sally Ann looked embarrassed by the applause while Mo nudged her companionably and flashed her broad white grin.

Pete went on, "I hope you've all had a chance to look around, and that you're as pleased as we are with the way everything turned out. Don't forget the meeting rooms are free to any club or civic group to use. You just have to register with Ms. Dillon's office first. The same for the activities center at the back of the building. We're going to have after school programs there, lectures, even yoga three times a week. None of this would have been possible without the genius of our county administrator, Margaret Dillon, who somehow managed to find the funding for all this without raising taxes much at all…" A few good-natured groans went around the room before Pete added, "… as well as every single member of the community who volunteered their time and their labor to make this dream a reality."

There were more cheers and applause, lasting longer this time, and when it died down Pete's voice had sobered. "The irony is that this whole project started out as a way to move the police station from that little closet they had downtown into larger quarters, and yet the police station was the last part of the project to be completed. But it's also appropriate, because it gives us a chance to celebrate today the men and women of law enforcement who put their lives on the line for all of us in a very real way this past year." He raised his glass to each person as he spoke the name. "Chief Aggie Malone. Officer Maureen Wilson. Sheriff Jerome Bishop. Captain Ryan Grady. And Officer Flash." He smiled as he said this and everyone chuckled, but his tone was heavy as he added, "And Officer Sam Brown, who made the ultimate sacrifice for the people of this community. Thank you all for your service. It will never be forgotten."

Flash sat up straight as the applause rang out, holding his head high. Aggie stood straight-shouldered beside him, and Flash saw Grady squeeze her fingers briefly. Flash could smell Aggie's salty tears, the kind she refused to let escape her eyes, but he wasn't alarmed. He had learned, over the four short years of his life, that people shed tears for a variety of reasons, not just because they were sad or in pain.

Besides, Grady had explained to him that they had to be patient with Aggie, now that their baby was on the way, because she was likely to be crying for reasons neither one of them understood. That was okay. Sometimes Flash felt like crying, too. But not today. Today he felt fierce, and proud, and glad to be alive.

The applause seemed to get louder by the minute, and it might have gone on forever if Pete hadn't raised his hand, beckoning people to be quiet. When he was able to be heard again, Pete said, "Before I turn you over to Father Dave for the dedication prayer and official ribbon cutting—y'all be sure to hang around for that—I just want to say one more thing."

He glanced down at his cup of sparkling cider, gathering his thoughts. "When I was a kid," he said, looking up, "my dad used to tell me all sorts of stories about what he called 'island resiliency. ' He talked about our ancestors fighting off Indian attacks, and about the plague that wiped out all but two dozen people on the whole island. He told how islanders swam out to rescue cargo from a sinking ship during the Civil War, and how the island was bombed—by our own people—during World War Two. Then there was the hurricane that virtually cut the island in half and created the lagoon that we call prime property today..." There were a few chuckles while Pete reminded them, "That was only one of fourteen Category 5 hurricanes that have hit the island since we've been keeping records. My dad used to say, 'our spirit cracked, but it was never broken. '"

He looked out over the crowd somberly. "This

winter," he said, "our spirit was severely cracked. I know that a lot of you thought about giving up. What the hell was the point, anyway? Life here is too hard. Why not start over in Tampa or Miami or Bermuda, for God's sake?" He paused and looked out over the crowd. "You are here today because you made a different choice, and I want to thank you for staying. Jason and Brett, thank you. Tom, Lester, Jeff, Ellie, Chesley, Lars, Tommy, Millie and Wes, Bobby, Randy..." His gaze fell, and lingered, on Aggie. "Aggie Malone... thank you for staying. We were cracked but not broken, and you all are the definition of island resiliency. So raise your glass, please, to yourselves, and to the future of Dogleg Island!"

The roar of approval from the crowd was so electric that Flash felt his fur prickle and stand on end, and it was all he could do to maintain his composure. While everyone was clapping and cheering, Aggie hugged Pete hard and said, "I know this isn't appropriate while I'm in uniform, but I trust you not to grab my gun. You give a hell of a speech, Pete!"

To which Pete grinned and kissed her cheek. "Love you, too, sis."

That prompted Grady to say, "Wait, he gets to kiss you and I don't?"

Aggie replied by bumping his shoulder with her own and saying, "If only you had your brother's gift of gab."

That made them all laugh, and it seemed a long time before the high spirits in the room calmed enough for Father Dave to step forward and say, "My friends, let us pray."

Father Dave's prayers were never long and hardly ever boring; nonetheless, Flash had learned it was considered rude to fall asleep during them. He therefore did not lower his head and close his eyes like everyone else in the room did, and that was how he happened to be the only one to see the stranger at the door.

The door was open into the hallway, and the man stopped on the threshold, looking startled to see so many people inside. He had brownish hair that was thin on top and tied in a ponytail in back with three different elastic bands, each one about an inch apart. Flash, whose border-collie genetics had programmed him to be a keen observer of details like that, found this fascinating. Sometimes Sally Ann tied sparkly ribbons at the end of her pigtails, or even jingle bells at Christmastime, but Flash had never known a man to do that.

He wore a green checked shirt and a leather bag on a long strap across his body, which Flash found interesting because he hardly ever saw men carrying bags like that around here. He wasn't dressed like a tourist and he didn't smell like suntan oil, and the way his eyes darted around the room, stopping only when they landed on Aggie, made Flash think the man had business with the police. Flash nosed Aggie's hand to get her attention, but Father Dave was still praying, and she merely stroked Flash's ear in response. At any rate, it didn't matter, because when Flash looked back toward the door, the stranger was gone.

Flash thought about following him, but he didn't like to interrupt Father Dave's prayer. In retrospect, maybe he should have, but it probably wouldn't have made a difference. Then again, maybe it would have.

You just never know how these things might turn out.

CHAPTER FIVE

T he ribbon was cut, the photographs were taken, and the business owners went to prepare for another day. A few people lingered in the reception room—Sheriff Bishop, Margaret Dillon, a few of the council members, all talking with authority about one thing or another, but it was a workday for most of the attendees. Aggie hugged Lorraine and thanked her repeatedly, but Lorraine brushed off the praise.

"You know I loved every minute of it," she said, beaming. "Besides, it was a group effort. Now, don't forget we have a family video chat with the folks at 8:00 tonight."

Aggie kept her expression pleasant with an effort. "The whole family?"

"I know, I know." Lorraine made a face. "These things are chaos when Lucy gets on with the twins, but maybe she'll put them to bed early tonight."

Lucy was Pete and Ryan's sister, the middle child of the Grady clan and the least popular. Her naturally abrasive personality was only exacerbated by her two ill-behaved seven-year-old boys and, as a recent divorcee, she had no shame about playing the victim card as often as she could.

Aggie sighed. "Well," she said, "I do love Lil and Salty, and it'll be nice to see them even if nobody can get a word in edgewise over the twins."

"That's the spirit." Lorraine gave her an encouraging grin. "Listen, I've got to get back to the bar and help Pete set up for the lunch crowd. Congratulations, Aggie. Everything turned out great, just like you pictured it."

Grady placed his hand lightly on Aggie's back. "As a citizen of Dogleg Island, I wouldn't mind seeing where my tax dollars went. How about a tour of the chief's new office?"

Lorraine blew a kiss to Aggie. "That's my cue. Don't work too hard, now." To Grady she added, "Video call, 8:00. Don't forget."

He replied, "Right." But the way he said it assured Aggie he had no idea what Lorraine was talking about.

"Your *folks*," Aggie reminded him as they walked toward her office. "We set it up last week, remember?"

"Right," he repeated, and Aggie didn't even bother rolling her eyes.

Flash reached the door to the office before them and opened the French handle with one swipe of his paws. When Aggie and Grady arrived at the threshold, he was stretched out in his new dog bed, paws in the air, luxuriating in the smell of new foam and plaid wool.

Grady chuckled. "I'd say he approves of his new digs."

Flash, having shown off the most important part of the new office, spun to his feet and assumed his position in front of the window, keeping an eye on the passersby. He knew when it was appropriate to play, and when it was time to work. This was a work day.

"What's not to approve?" Aggie stretched out her arms, delighted. This was the first time she'd seen the space fully furnished, and she couldn't have been more pleased. Sally Ann and Mo had been responsible for moving everything out of their old quarters over the weekend, and the pieces of furniture Aggie had picked out had been delivered while she was banned from the premises due to paint fumes. "Oh, Ryan, it's just perfect."

"It was kind of hard to screw up," he replied, "since you only drew us about two dozen diagrams."

The room was easily twice the size of the entire former police station, which actually wasn't saying much. There was a navy-blue love seat with a subtle sea gull pattern, and a couple of straight-backed guest chairs. Aggie's desk was in front of the window, with Flash's bed and silver water bowl behind it. There was even a mini fridge and a coffee maker, which was a nice thought even though Aggie was off coffee for the next six months, at least. The oil painting of Flash that Ryan had commissioned hung over the desk. A framed photo from their Christmas wedding was on her desk.

"And here"—Aggie framed the space beside the love seat with a sweep of her arms—"is where I'll put the playpen when little Lilly is old enough to come to work with me."

At his skeptical look she objected, "What? This is Dogleg Island, not the NYPD."

"Not that," he said. "But Lilly? Are you sure? I love my mom, but I'm not a fan of flower names."

She looked mildly uncertain. "Let me think about it."

Then Aggie smiled and draped her arms around his neck. "Thanks for this, Ry. Not just for everything you did to get us here, but for patrolling Beachside Park when you're off duty and not even telling me about it, and sending deputies over here on all kinds of pretenses just so we'd have extra man power during tourist season, and letting me sleep late and making breakfast and, well, everything."

He smiled. "You're worth it," he assured her and kissed her.

While they talked, and inevitably kissed, Flash made some interesting observations from the window. There was Mr. McMasters, the gardener, sitting on the bench by the harbor sidewalk, feeding the remnants of his sausage biscuit to the seagulls that swooped down to take the scraps from his fingers. Amazing, how they did that. He held up a piece of biscuit to the sky, and there came a seagull, snatching it out of his fingers like they'd choreographed the whole thing. Some tourists stopped to take pictures. A squirrel crept along the railing next to the seawall, probably looking to steal a crumb or two for himself. Flash felt a bark rising in his throat but thought better of it. After all, if he barked at every squirrel he saw, he wouldn't have time to do anything else.

A woman with a baby in a carriage jogged by, talking on her phone, and the seagulls scattered. And then, most interestingly of all, the man in the green checked shirt walked by, right in front of the window. He looked neither right nor left, holding his leather bag close to his hip, walking with a long purposeful stride. Mr. McMasters turned his head to watch him go by, and so did Flash. Flash hardly ever saw a stranger twice in such a short space of time in this part of town. Most tourists—and there weren't that many left in late September—could be found beachside or in the downtown cluster of shops and restaurants. It was curious.

After a moment, the gardener got up, dusted the last of the biscuit crumbs from his jeans, and moved off in the same direction the man in the green checked shirt had gone. The woman with the baby carriage turned toward town, out of Flash's frame of view. A teenager came by, bouncing a basketball, and Flash's ears pricked forward. Basketball was one of his favorite games.

There was a light knock on the doorframe and Sally Ann said, "Excuse me, Chief, but..." She broke off, blushing, and looked uncertain whether to stay or go. "Oh, um..."

Grady chuckled as Aggie stepped back quickly, straightening her hair with her fingers. "It's okay, Sally Ann," he assured her. "We're married."

Aggie added, "It's fine. What's up?"

Sally Ann smoothed the folds of her skirt nervously. "It's Ms. Kidd in the records office. She wants you to come down when you have a minute. She seemed upset."

"Tell her I'll be right there."

Sally Ann left, tactfully pulling the door closed behind her.

Grady kissed Aggie's nose lightly. "I've got to get to work, and so do you. The chief is taking the morning off. I guess you can do that when you're sheriff."

Aggie said, "Take some cake with you for the guys in the office. And be careful in this heat."

"You, too. Have a great day, sweetheart."

Grady paused at the door. "Hey, Flash."

Flash looked around.

Grady pointed two fingers toward his eyes, and then toward Aggie. Flash grinned his acknowledgement. It was a familiar signal between them. *Watch over Aggie.* Like he would ever do anything else.

CHAPTER SIX

The tax records office was located at the back of the building down the hall from the island administrator's office. The place looked completely different than it had the last time Aggie had been here. Its walls were painted a soft blue, lighthouse paintings and vintage photographs of Dogleg Island decorated the corridor, and a nice, slate gray carpet covered the floor. Still, Aggie felt her throat tighten the minute she made the turn into that part of the building, trying hard not to hear the sound of breaking glass, the explosion of gunfire, the thunder of choppers overhead. This is where it had all happened... for her, anyway, and Grady and Flash. She had to stop for a moment, swallowing hard, afraid she might actually be sick.

Flash leaned against her, thinking about memories, and how strange it was that sometimes remembering something could hurt more than the actual thing that caused the remembering. The thrumming of helicopters sounded louder, the screams more terrifying, the gunfire sharper. The blood that covered Aggie's dress and splashed on her face. The bad man that held a gun to her head. Lights cutting through the dark, swirling overhead. Men shouting orders. That had been an awful, awful night. But remembering it was somehow even worse.

Aggie took a deep breath, then another. She squared her shoulders and moved on, Flash at her side.

Voices from the remnants of the party still echoed down the hallway, but most everyone had to open up their businesses by 9:00, including Margaret Dillon. Aggie and Flash tried to move quickly and quietly past the open door of her office, but no such luck. She was standing behind her desk, sorting through some file folders, and looked up as Aggie passed.

"Chief Malone, a minute?"

Aggie hesitated, "I'm actually on my way..."

"Then I'll be brief," she interrupted briskly. "You've had six months to replace Officer Brown, and unless you do so before the end of the year, you're going to lose your funding. Sorry to be blunt, but given the expenses of the past year, the treasury can make good use of the money if you're not going to spend it. Kindly let me know your decision." She turned back to sorting the folders. "And welcome to the building."

Aggie took that to mean she was dismissed. Aggie and Flash proceeded down the corridor, where Geraldine Kidd was waiting outside her office.

"I tried not to touch anything," Geraldine said nervously when they reached her, "although I probably did. Or maybe it's nothing. I mean I hate to bother you if it is, but it's probably nothing, don't you think, Chief?"

Geraldine Kidd was a woman in her mid-sixties who wore her gray hair in a French twist and dressed in no-nonsense khaki trousers and a white blouse every day for work—except during the winter, when she switched to dark wool trousers. She had been in charge of the island's property and tax records for close to forty years, a dull, featureless job that she did with exceptional competence. Aggie had never even seen her rattled before, much less as anxious as she appeared now.

"What happened?" Aggie asked.

"It's probably my fault," Geraldine said, twisting her hands together. "I might have left the door unlocked. But I *always* lock up, and I just can't imagine leaving here over the weekend without double-checking the lock. But when I came to open up a few minutes ago, you know, after the party broke up, the door was standing open and, well..." She gestured them helplessly inside.

The office was comprised of two rooms. They entered the smaller, outer office where Geraldine's desk was located and found all her desk drawers open with papers, pens, and personal items scattered across the top or spilled onto the floor.

"Is anything missing?" Aggie asked.

"Not that I could tell," she said. "I even had a five-dollar bill and a handful of quarters in the top drawer, and they're still there."

Aggie looked around the room. The door to the file room was open, the keys still in the lock. She said, "You keep the keys to the file room in your drawer, right?"

She nodded. "That's what I wanted to show you. I *know* the file room door was locked. It locks automatically when you close it. But it was standing open when I got here, and…" she led the way to the file room. "Someone had definitely been here."

This was one room that had not been renovated since Aggie had been here last. The overhead fluorescents cast an eerie glow over the floor-to-ceiling rows of filing cabinets and shelves filled with dusty bank boxes and oversized plat books. Everything from maps to building plans to deeds and sales records were stored here, going back at least a hundred years. There was even a file drawer of birth certificates from the sixties when Dogleg Island had its own maternity hospital. Although Dogleg Island was technically a part of Murphy County, it had always done its own recordkeeping and, for the most part, its own governing. That sense of independence and contempt for outside authority was still evident among the islanders today.

Aggie came into the room and Flash followed, nose to the ground, doing his usual careful search for evidence. The first thing Aggie noticed was that a box of deeds had been removed from a shelf and placed on the long table that bisected the room. She said, "Did you check the box for missing documents?"

Geraldine shook her head adamantly. "No, ma'am.

I went straight to your office to report a crime. Like I said, I didn't want to disturb anything."

Aggie smiled at her reassuringly and went to examine the box. The label said, "Property Deeds, 1975-1982." Each year had a manila folder, clearly marked in Geraldine's hand, and they all appeared to be in chronological order. Except 1979 and 1980 were missing. Aggie checked twice to be sure.

"Is there any other place these files could be?" she asked Geraldine. "Another box, maybe?"

"Goodness, no," the other woman replied. She sounded mildly insulted. "I'm very meticulous about my files and that box hasn't been touched in years."

Aggie gave her a reassuring smile and noticed that Flash was paying particular attention to something he had found on the floor. She went over and picked up a green elastic ponytail band with a green bead. She held it up to Geraldine. "Is this yours?"

She shook her head. "And the last person who was in here besides me was Ralph Waters, looking for his property tax record from three years ago. That was last week."

Flash, of course, knew exactly where the band had come from, and why the man in the green checked shirt had been hanging around during Father Dave's prayer, then had been hurrying along the sidewalk afterwards. What had transpired in between those times was still to be determined, but the things that weren't yet known were what made their jobs—his and Aggie's—so interesting.

Aggie tucked the elastic band into her pocket and

went back out into the hallway to examine the lock. "Well, you can set your mind at ease about leaving the door unlocked," she told Geraldine. She pointed out the nicks and scratches in the faceplate. "This lock has been jimmied, probably with a flathead screwdriver and a credit card. These locks are pretty easy to manipulate that way."

She cast her gaze around the office once again. "They broke in, ransacked your desk for the keys to the file room, and then stole the deeds for the years 1979 and 1980."

"But why?" Geraldine looked both perplexed and despairing, as though she blamed herself somehow for this failure of the system. "We're open 9:00 to 5:00 every weekday, and our records are available on request. All you have to do is fill out a form and show ID. It takes less than a minute."

"Maybe they didn't want to do the paperwork," suggested Aggie. She gestured to the lock. "Call a locksmith and get this replaced. There's a good one in Ocean City, Security One. They come out the same day. I'll write up a report and send a copy over to the city manager so you can be reimbursed for the expense."

Geraldine looked anxious. "You don't think... I mean, you don't suppose there's any chance that they would come back, do you?"

Aggie said firmly, "No, ma'am, I don't. I think whoever it was got what they wanted and will be on their way. I'll open an investigation, but in the meantime, you're perfectly safe here."

Geraldine's shoulders sagged with visible relief,

then she smiled. "Well, it sure is good to have police in the building, I'll tell you that much."

Aggie managed to smile back. "Yes, ma'am. We're glad to be here too."

Unfortunately she wasn't entirely sure that was true.

CHAPTER SEVEN

Aggie made it halfway back to her office before the nausea overwhelmed her. She bolted to the ladies' room and threw up in the toilet. The episode was over as quickly as it had begun, and she splashed water on her face, not much liking the reflection she saw in the mirror as she patted her face dry with a paper towel. The woman who looked back was pasty-faced and puffy-eyed, straight black hair feathering across her cheekbones and catching in the moisture around her eyes. She took a breath, squared her shoulders, and finger-combed her hair. "Okay," she whispered. "Get yourself together. It's a workday."

Flash was waiting patiently when she came out, and so was Mo. Mo's broad dark face was creased with concern as she said, "You okay, honey?"

"Morning sickness," Aggie said. "It comes and goes." Although the truth was, she thought the nausea had less to do with morning sickness than with the simple fact of being back here again.

Mo put a comforting hand on her shoulder as they

walked back to the office, Flash trotting alongside. "I left a bag of ginger candies in your desk," she said. "You just keep sucking on them, fix you right up."

"Thanks, Mo," Aggie said, "I will." Then, "Geraldine Kidd's office was broken into over the weekend."

"Huh." Mo frowned. "They get anything?"

"A couple of file folders with property deeds from 1979 and 80."

Mo shook her head with an expression that was part disdain and part disbelief. "The things people will do."

"You got that right."

There were only a few people left in the office as Aggie, Mo, and Flash returned. Sheriff Bishop was talking to one of the council members, and two of the members of the garden club were lingering over cake and coffee, catching up on gossip. Sally Ann cast them covert impatient looks from behind her desk, clearly wishing they would leave so she could get back to work.

Aggie, glancing at Sally Ann's pigtails, dug the elastic band out of her pocket and showed it to her. "Is this yours?"

Sally Ann shook her head. "No, ma'am. Those will break your hair and give you split ends. I use the braided kind. Sheriff Bishop wanted to know when you got back but..." She looked across the room. "Looks like he's busy now."

"In that case," Mo said meaningfully, "you got a minute to talk before I go out on patrol?"

Aggie forced another smile. "Sure thing."

Aggie took a seat behind her desk and added, "But if you tell me you're leaving, I'm going to burst into tears and it'll be all your fault."

The big woman chuckled and eased herself into the chair. She barely fit, and the chair creaked alarmingly. "Now, whatever would give you a fool notion like that?"

Flash relaxed as Mo gave him a quick tug of the ears and settled back. One thing was for sure, Mo was the one person you could count on not to burst into tears for no reason. When Mo was around, things were almost always under control. Flash felt comfortable going back to his post by the window.

Mo was 350 pounds if she was an ounce, ebony-skinned, ferociously made. She was a former prison guard who'd been known to render a suspect helpless with one swipe of her baton—completely justified, of course—and in the next moment wriggle halfway into a sewer pipe to rescue a terrified kitten. If she had not agreed to leave the sheriff's department to work on Dogleg Island, Aggie was not entirely sure she would have taken the police chief's job. She and Mo had been a team since the day the department was formed. Through all the challenges they had faced over the past few years—and there had been plenty—Aggie had always known she could count on Mo.

Nonetheless, Aggie's muscles tensed as Mo's expression grew severe. She folded her hands across her ample abdomen and said, "But I got something to say and I'm gonna say it straight."

Aggie mentally braced herself. "I expect nothing

less."

"Now, I'm not telling you anything you don't already know," Mo went on brusquely. "We managed fine over the summer with the sheriff's office helping out, I don't deny that, but you know it would've been a lot easier with an extra man. And with that baby coming you've got no business running all over this island breaking up fights and hauling in drunks, not to mention working all hours of the night when you should be at home taking care of yourself—and your family. I know it's hard, thinking about replacing that boy. But things are changing, whether you like it or not, and you've got to keep up. You need to get another officer in here and you need to do it now." She fixed Aggie with a stern look, concluding firmly, "I've said my piece. You take it or leave it."

Aggie sighed. "I know. The island is growing; that's why I asked for an extra officer in the first place. I'm not going to be able to put in the kind of hours I used to, and I'm already over budget with the sheriff's department. Grady is working unpaid overtime doing beach patrol before and after shift. I have to make a decision. But Mo, you've seen the kind of applicants we've been getting and…"

"You leave that to me," Mo said firmly. "You give me warm body and I'll whip 'em into shape."

"If only it was that easy," Aggie said. But even as she spoke, she wondered if Mo was right. Was she putting off replacing Sam for all the wrong reasons?

Sally Ann's voice came through the intercom on Aggie's desk. Aggie jumped a little, startled. She was accustomed to glancing three feet across the room to find Sally Ann and had never even had to raise her voice to be heard.

"Excuse me, Chief," Sally Ann said, "but we have a request for a welfare check on Grace Henderson, Number 12 Swallowtail Place. Her daughter called from Ohio and said she'd missed their usual Sunday afternoon phone call, and she hasn't heard from her since. And Sheriff Bishop wants to know if you're free."

"I got it," Mo said, hauling herself to her feet. She added sternly, "You think about what I said."

Aggie smiled at her gratefully and said into the intercom. "Tell Sheriff Bishop to come in."

As Mo left, Aggie glanced over her shoulder at Flash and murmured, "Mondays, am I right?"

Flash swiped his tail across the floor in happy agreement.

Jerome Bishop was a six-foot-tall, broad-shouldered Black man who took up every inch of a room in which he entered. His crew cut was graying, the lines around his eyes were weathered, but the power of his presence had not diminished since he had first been elected sheriff of Murphy County over thirty years ago. Aggie stood automatically when he came in because, well, that's what a person did.

He spread his arms and smiled as he looked around the new office. "Now, *this* is more like it, eh, Chief?"

Aggie came around the desk, grinning as she extended her hands. "You'd better believe it. Almost as fancy as yours."

He squeezed her fingers and kissed her cheek, and when Flash trotted over, he bent to give him a good scratch under the chin. Flash had known Bishop almost as long as he'd known Aggie, and the sheriff was one of his favorite people. They went fishing together with Grady, and when Bishop came to their house for dinner, he always shared his catch with Flash. He was family.

Bishop took a seat on the new navy love seat and Aggie wheeled her desk chair around to sit across from him. Flash went back to his post by the window. He could still hear everything that was said, but he didn't want to miss any of the sights, either. And sure enough, in the short time he'd been gone, one of the stray cats that liked to roam the harbor front had crept up and scattered the seagulls that were still looking for random crumbs on the sidewalk.

Aggie and Bishop chatted for a few minutes about the new building and the ribbon cutting, and how nice the surprise party had been. Then Aggie said, only half-joking, "I don't suppose you have a deputy you want to get rid of, do you? One who'd like to come work at the beach for about half pay and almost no benefits?"

The sheriff chuckled. "You'd think that'd be an easy ask, wouldn't you? But I'm afraid not. I can hardly recruit them myself." Then he added, "But I do have something along those lines I'd like you think about, now that you brought it up."

Aggie said cautiously, "Okay."

Bishop went on, "You know, when I agreed to

come out of retirement and accept the appointment as Murphy County sheriff, it was only until the next election. Well, the next election is coming up, and I don't intend to run."

Aggie sat back heavily in her chair. "Oh," she said. It was hard to imagine Murphy County without Sheriff Bishop, and she hadn't realized his term was so nearly up. "But," she said, "no one else is on the ballot. We all just assumed…"

"The deadline to file for a county election is still five days away," he assured her. "And there are a couple of boys running, just nobody you've ever heard of." He paused and ran a hand over his short-cropped hair. "Truth is, Aggie, it was a lot harder to make the decision than I thought it would be, which is why I put it off so long. I know everybody figured I'd run again, and up to a point, so did I. But…" he smiled wryly. "I'm a lot closer to seventy than I was when I took the job two years ago, and I hope I've got a little more sense. It's time to step down."

She frowned, still unsettled. "But… what will you do?"

He chuckled again. "As little as possible," he assured her. "A little fishing, a little gardening. And, I hope, a lot of babysitting when that little one of yours gets here."

She said uncertainly, "It sure is going to be hard, getting used to having someone else in your office."

"Maybe not," he said. He leaned forward and held her gaze. "I want Grady to take the job."

She stared at him.

Before she could speak, he raised a hand to stall her. "I know, I know. I had the same idea the last time I retired, and he wouldn't consider it. But a lot has changed since then, not the least of which is Ryan Grady. I know he could win an election. He's got the name, the personality, the record… and my endorsement, naturally. It'd be a lot more money, Aggie," he went on, "and you can use it now that you're starting a family. A lot of responsibility, it's true, but the hours are what you make them, so he could be home weekends, four weeks' vacation a year… not a bad job, all things considered."

Aggie was still a little disoriented. "Have you mentioned this to Ryan?"

"Without getting you onboard first?" He shook his head. "I've known Ryan Grady all his life, and the last time he did something you didn't want him to was before he met you. So I want you to think about it, talk it over, decide what you both think is best for your family. But…" He braced his hands on his knees and stood up. "Do it quick. Filing deadline is Friday."

When he was gone, Aggie gave a little shake of her head as though trying to clear it, but she did not get up. "Well, Flash," she murmured, "what do you think about that?"

But Flash didn't have time to think anything about it. He heard the ringing of the 911 dispatch line from Sally Ann's desk, and he was already racing toward the door. After all, that's what made his job so interesting. You just never knew what was going to happen next.

CHAPTER EIGHT

Donny Keller was waiting outside the hardware store when Aggie and Flash pulled up. His skinny arms were folded over his chest and a ferocious scowl knotted his salt-and-pepper eyebrows. Flash bounded out of the open window of their patrol vehicle as soon as it stopped and began to sniff the premises for evidence. Aggie got out more slowly, using her eyes to do the same job. Donny Keller strode forward before she had even closed the door.

"I'm telling you, Chief, this is the last damn straw," he said angrily. "Three times—*three times*—in one year I've been broke into, and what are you going to do about it? Huh?"

Aggie noted the front door appeared to be secure, the "Closed" sign still in place, and the dusty display of fishing tackle and camping gear in the front window was undisturbed. The flaking Keller's Hardware sign hung crookedly over the door, just as it had for the past fifteen years.

"How'd they get in?"

"Broke the lock on the back door," he responded in a growl.

Flash had already discovered this. His explorations had led him around the building, where spikes of dying grass poked their way through the crushed shell parking lot and the wheels of heavy trucks had left ruts beside the dumpster. He smelled rotting garbage and cat pee and lizards baking in the sun, shoe leather and human sweat and shrimp from the bait shop next door. On top of all that, faint but fresh, was the iron-bitter trace scent of blood.

The scarred wooden door at the back hung open crookedly on its hinges, and a chunk of wood had been gouged out of the frame along with the barrel lock. It was there that Flash found the smear of blood, right along the jagged metal edge of the faceplate, and another drop in the sand below the door. After a little more exploring, Flash found the crowbar that had pried open the lock hidden in the weeds about eight feet away. It, too, had a smear of blood on it. He went back to report to Aggie.

Aggie walked with Donny toward the back of the building, meeting Flash halfway there. She said, "You know, Donny, I told you last time you need to replace that door with a good strong security door. Sitting back here up against a vacant lot with no security lighting makes you an easy target."

He scowled even more fiercely, "Yeah, I know what you told me."

"At a certain point your insurance is going to stop covering your claims."

"Not my fault if law enforcement can't keep the criminals behind bars and protect the honest businessman," he shot back.

The truth was, Aggie suspected that the previous two so-called burglaries had been committed by Donny Keller himself, for the insurance money. In January, two generators and a tractor mower had gone missing, retail value $4,650. Four months later a hundred feet of 4-inch copper tubing valued at $5,500 had disappeared. None of the merchandise had been recovered, but high-end items like tractor mowers were not something one would typically expect to find at Keller's hardware, and within days of delivery they had been stolen. Aggie also couldn't help noticing that three weeks after that, Donny was driving a new truck.

Aggie pulled on a pair of gloves from her back pocket and examined the broken door handle. Flash stood close, but not so close as to get in the way. "Looks like our day for B&Es, huh, Flash?" she remarked.

Flash had noticed that things sometimes happened like that in police work. Aggie called them patterns. Sometimes those patterns were important; sometimes they were just things that happened. But Aggie said they always needed to pay attention to them, just in case.

Aggie straightened up from examining the broken door. "Looks like he had a little accident while breaking in," she observed, pointing out the blood. "Was the door open when you got here?"

"Just like you found it."

Flash waited patiently for her to look around for the crowbar, and when she did, he led her the few feet into the weeds where it lay. She took a picture with her phone, and then picked it up with a gloved hand. "Is this yours?" she asked Donny.

"Not unless he stole it from my store," Donny replied belligerently.

Aggie examined the pits and scars on the crowbar, along with the blood smear. "It doesn't look new."

"You think that's what they used to break in?" Donny demanded.

"Probably."

She pushed open the door and walked in, Flash at her side. The overhead fluorescents were already on, revealing a small room crowded with shelves, the shelves packed with haphazardly arranged merchandise. A stack of lawnmower tires blocked one aisle; a couple of porcelain sinks leaned against the back wall. Everything looked dusty and greasy and smelled like neglect. Donny was always complaining he couldn't compete with the big box stores across the bridge, and this was why. Aggie didn't know anyone who shopped here anymore. Even Grady said it was cheaper to drive across the bridge for a quart of motor oil than to buy it here.

Aggie said, "Is this the way you come in to unlock the store every morning?"

He frowned in annoyance. "You know it is. You asked me that last time."

She stayed where she was by the door, continuing

to look around. Flash remained at her side, wondering if she had noticed the shoe prints on the sticky floor, pointing inward. There were two sets. One clearly belonged to Donny Keller's flip-flops, with their distinctive round circle at the toe. The other set was bigger and belonged to a pair of sneakers. There were other prints and scuffs, too, but you didn't have to possess Flash's superior sense of smell to realize these were the freshest. And they were the only ones leading from the back door inside.

Aggie remarked, "Still no security cameras, huh?"

"Do you know how much those things cost?"

"You can get a simple home-security system for under $500."

He just grunted.

Aggie looked at his flip-flops, then at the prints on the floor. She took out her phone and snapped a picture of the floor, just in case. Flash, no longer concerned about smudging the evidence, began to sniff ahead, following the footprints and the scent of blood.

Aggie walked over to the cabinet where Donny kept the ammunition, gave the roll-down metal cover a shake, and found it secure. She looked back over her shoulder at him. "So what did they get?"

"Near as I can tell," he responded, folding his arms over his chest again, "nothing but a roll of det cord."

She was startled, and he saw it. "Detonation cord? You're sure?"

"Yeah, I thought that'd get your attention." His tone was smug. "Somebody breaks into a place and steals explosives, you gotta think they're up to no good, am I right?"

Flash's ears pricked at that, and he turned his head to better observe the conversation. He knew a little about explosives, having helped Aggie uncover the body of a man who had blown a hole in the ground with them. That place had smelled nothing like this, though. That place had smelled like lightning in a storm and burned earth and the pellets that made flowers grow. This place smelled like mold and old boxes and things with oil in their parts. He listened more carefully, trying to understand.

Aggie said, "Show me where it is."

"Was," he corrected bitterly. "Where it *was*." He led the way toward the corner where Flash was already waiting. "I shoulda known something was up yesterday when that guy called."

"What guy?"

"How should I know what guy? If I knew, I'd tell you, wouldn't I? He wanted to know if I had any det cord, and I told him I had a spool of about twenty feet left over from when they were clearing out the lagoon after the hurricane, and I'd let him have it for a hundred bucks. He said he didn't want to pay that much but thanks anyway, and hung up." He snorted. "Guess he found it at a price he could afford."

Aggie glanced at him. "Your license to sell explosive materials is up to date, right?"

He scowled back at her. "I didn't call you out here to start questioning my credentials."

Aggie decided to let it go. Donny Keller had been

providing local contractors and homeowners with small quantities of low-grade explosives for years, saving them the time and effort of ordering from out-of-state suppliers. As far as Aggie knew, no one had ever questioned his qualifications to do so except herself, and the last time she had checked two years ago his license had been valid.

He stopped in front of a jumble of wheelbarrows, shovels, and rolls of hardware cloth. A couple of cement bags were broken open on the floor, and a container of rebar had been turned over, its contents scattered across the floor. There was another, very clear footprint in the cement dust on the floor, and Aggie took a careful photo of it.

Donny said, "I kept it back here, kind of between the rebar and the cement. Don't know why he had to make such a damn mess."

Aggie figured, with the haphazard way merchandise was stacked, the perpetrator hadn't had much choice.

She said, "And you're sure nothing else was taken?"

"Not that I can see. I probably wouldn't even have noticed the spool was missing," he admitted, "not for a while anyway, if he hadn't turned everything upside down back here."

"Well, keep looking, will you?" Aggie said. "Do you have caller ID on your phone?"

Keller led her to the landline behind the counter, and Aggie scrolled back through the list of calls that had come in within the past seventy-two hours. It was as sad a testament to a failing business as she had ever seen. There were only five calls. Three were from Donny's wife, one from a supplier, and the other from a blocked number. That, of course, would be the man she was looking for.

Aggie made notes, took more photos, bagged the crowbar as evidence, and told Donny to call her if he discovered anything else missing. She left him with a stern warning to replace the back door with something sturdier, and a strong suggestion that he invest in security cameras. Then she and Flash went back outside to look around some more.

Keller's Hardware was located on Island Drive near the bridge, in the older part of Dogleg Island that most businesses had abandoned. There was a liquor store that still did good business, and a convenience/quick grocery store where tourists stopped to stock up on whatever they had forgotten to buy at the supermarket across the bridge. Both of those businesses had security cameras, but they were facing the wrong way to be of much help in this case. Next door to Keller's was Shipwreck Bait & Tackle, which had been a fixture on Dogleg Island since before Grady was born. It did not have security cameras, but it had a proprietor who knew everything and everyone on Dogleg. Flash and Aggie walked across the sandy path to the shop.

CHAPTER NINE

Next to Pete's Place Bar and Grille—and maybe the maritime museum upstairs in the Grady warehouse building—Shipwreck Bait & Tackle was Flash's favorite place on the whole island. He came there often with Grady and Bishop, and while they were joking and telling stories—and sometimes drinking beer—with old Mr. Obadiah, Flash would explore the cave of wonder that was the Shipwreck. There were crabs scuttling around in a big wire case, and live shrimp floating in sea water. There was a giant tortoise—almost as big as Flash himself—sitting on a stool, but it wasn't alive. Likewise, a big blue fish that had once been alive but was no longer soared along one wall. The plank floors smelled like brine and old varnish, and there was a display of shiny fishing lures on the counter that fluttered in the breeze from the window air conditioner and cast patterns of light across the walls. Flash could have spent hours looking at that display, but he never did. There was always too much else to explore.

Flash raced ahead of Aggie and pushed open the door. A bell clanged as he wriggled through before the door could close again, and Mr. Obadiah grinned at him from behind the counter. "Well, now, Mr. Flash," he greeted him, "fancy seeing you here bright and early this morning. How'd you like a nice piece of beef jerky to start your day out?"

Flash indicated that he'd like that just fine by placing his paws on the counter and taking the proffered piece of jerky politely from Mr. Obadiah's fingers. That, of course, was the other reason he liked coming here.

He had just finished up and was checking out the live crab case when Aggie came in. The bell jingled behind her, and Mr. Obadiah started pouring coffee over a cup of cracked ice. "Good morning, Chief. Do you think we're ever gonna get any rain?"

"No, sir," she replied frankly. "I don't."

"And here it is in the middle of storm season," he said. "Time was, we'd've had two or three Cat 2s hit the coast by now, at least."

"Climate change, Mr. Obadiah."

"I reckon. Can't say I care much for it, though. How about an iced coffee for you? Fresh made."

Aggie held up a hand in protest. "Thanks, but I'm off coffee for a while. We're expecting a baby in April," she told him.

Mr. Obadiah put down the coffee cup and braced his hands on the counter, smiling at her broadly. "Are you, now? Well, if that's not the best news I've heard in a coon's age!"

Obadiah Williams was a tall, light-skinned Black man of indeterminate age who had been a fixture on Dogleg Island since before the bridge was built. He sold everything from deep sea tackle to shrimp nets, fishing line and bait and hooks and lures of every conceivable variety. He knew where the fish were biting and what time of day; he knew the sandbars and reefs and the deep spots in the lagoon where the fish liked to hide beneath the roots of fallen trees. Everyone who came across the bridge with any intention of catching anything stopped at the Shipwreck. And everyone, tourist or native, with even so much as a casual interest in the sport knew Mr. Obadiah.

That was why Aggie had been so surprised to see the "For Sale" sign in the window as she came up the steps. She jerked a thumb backwards to it now. "You're not selling out, are you, Mr. Obadiah?"

"Yes'm," he acknowledged, his tone sobering. "I'm afraid it's come time. Fifty-six years I been holding down this countertop, and I got to tell you, I'm gettin' a might weary. Be eighty-seven next month, you know."

Aggie said in surprise, "No, I didn't know. You sure don't look it."

He chuckled and poured cream over the iced coffee. "Well, I feel it, I can tell you that, in ever' bone of my body. And to tell you the truth, I've made about all the money I care to. Time to take it easy for a while. My daughter, she's got a nice little unit picked out for me in this retirement village over in Ocean City—

maybe you know it; Whispering Pines?—and I figure I wouldn't mind having somebody fix my meals and do my laundry while I rock on the porch and tell my stories for whatever years I got left."

"Wow," Aggie said, giving a small shake of her head. "Well, we sure are going to miss you. It's hard to imagine this place without you."

His expression softened. "That's kind of you to say, Miss Aggie. Real kind. Now," he added more energetically, "what can I do for you this morning? You and the big guy"—he cast a wink at Flash —"thinking about casting out for redfish? I hear they're running out on the south end of the island, but you better not wait until the sun gets much higher."

Flash, his attention caught by the mention of fishing, abandoned his almost hypnotic study of shrimp floating in a bubbling aerator and returned to Aggie.

Aggie chuckled, "No, sir, this is a working day for me. It seems the hardware store was broken into last night, and I wonder if you might've seen or heard anything that might be helpful."

He shook his head thoughtfully. "No'm, not that strikes my mind. Of course, you know I can't really see anything from here except my own parking lot."

Aggie looked around and agreed. The only window that might have had a view of the hardware store was blocked by the AC unit, which also would have disguised the sound of wood splintering fifty yards away.

"I got here about 5:00 a. m. , like usual," Obadiah

went on, "and everything was as dark as can be. A little before 6:00 a young fella come in and bought a pack of 40-pound test, and after that the usual crowd—mainlanders buying bait, a couple of tourists stocking up their coolers, Jack Fielding needed a new live well... truth of the matter is, this is about the first break I've had all morning."

Aggie persisted, "But you can't think of anything that you might call suspicious?"

He thought about it. "Well, now, aside from the fella with the 40-pound, I can't think of a thing. I said to him, 'What're going use that for? Anything you hook in deep water's gonna break that right in two, and you try surfcasting with it you ain't gonna catch nothing but sand. He just shrugged and paid cash and went on about his business." He frowned. "Wait a minute. Maybe there is something. Fella had a scrape on the back of his hand. It looked fresh, still bleeding a little. I said, 'Do you want a bandage for that?'—you know I keep a first aid kit behind the counter, here, for folks that come in with scrapes and bites and fishhook wounds after a day on the water—but he said he was fine and left. Say, you don't suppose he might've gotten that scrape from breaking into Donny's store, do you?"

Flash's ears had pricked up at this, but Aggie kept her expression neutral. She was always professional, so Flash tried to be too.

Aggie took out her notebook. "Which hand was hurt?"

He scrunched up his face, picturing it. "Left one."

"What did he look like?"

"Oh, twenties, I'd say, crew cut, shorts and tee shirt. A little shorter than me, regular build. Gray shirt, I think, or maybe blue, with some kind of writing on it. Yellow shorts with orange on them, you know the kind kids wear. Sneakers, no socks. White guy." He gave a half grin. "Real white, starting to go red. Definitely not from around here."

"Tattoos? Scars, jewelry?"

"No, ma'am, nothing like that. Just the cut on his hand."

"Did you see what kind of vehicle he was driving?"

He shook his head thoughtfully. "Pickup truck, I can tell you that. Might've been gray, might've been green, might've been light blue... it was still dark you know, hard to tell."

"Did you see the license plate?"

"Sorry. Do you think that might've been him, Chief? Seems kind of crazy to break into a hardware store and then come in here to buy fishing line."

She smiled and put her notebook away. "Yeah, it does. Thanks for your help, Mr. Obadiah. You have a good day, now. And don't move away without letting us know. We'll throw you a party."

He chuckled. "You be sure and bring that baby over to see me when I get settled in my new place."

Aggie waved goodbye to him as she pushed open the door, and Flash trotted through before her.

"What do you think, Flash?" she said as they walked back across the sand toward their SUV, which was still parked in front of the hardware store. "Why *would* a man break into a hardware store to steal explosive cord, then drive next door to buy fishing line?"

Flash had no answer for that. He was not nearly as good at the why of things as he was at how and where, or even the who. It wasn't that he didn't find the whys interesting. He spent a lot of time turning them over in his head when people thought he was sleeping. Why did birds sing? Why did Grady yell at the little people on the television set and why did Aggie laugh at him when he did? Why did the changing of the world seem to make Mr. Obadiah and Aggie so sad when everybody knew that the way it changed was the best part about the world? Those were the things Flash would enjoy contemplating when he returned to his red plaid bed in the new office. As for why a bad guy would want to explode something and then go fishing, Flash had not the first idea. Of course, the most interesting thing about whys—at least in Flash's experience—was that the answers to them hardly ever made any difference in the end.

To Flash's relief, Aggie did not appear to be counting on him for the answer. Instead, she took out her phone and dialed Grady.

"Good morning, Chief," Grady answered, just as though he hadn't kissed her goodbye little more than an hour ago. "What can I do for you this fine day?"

Aggie said, "There was a break-in at Keller's Hardware last night. A spool of det cord was stolen, nothing else."

Grady returned a smothered groan. "And here I was

imagining you spending the day in your nice new air-conditioned office, learning how to operate the new copy machine."

She said, "We have a new copy machine?"

Grady grunted. "You sure this is not another one of Keller's scams?"

"Pretty sure. We traced what might be the suspect next door to Mr. Obadiah's, where he bought a pack of 40-pound test fishing line. White male, sunburned, crew cut, medium build, cut or scrape on his left hand. Driving a pickup truck of indeterminate color. I'll get the full report out to you when I get back to the office, but I thought the sheriff's office should be apprised."

"Crap," Grady muttered. "I hope it's not another crazy-ass treasure hunter planning to blow another damn hole in the island."

"Yeah, me, too." She sighed. Then, "Say, Ryan, did you know Mr. Obadiah is selling out?"

"No lie." He sounded surprised. "Well, that's something I never thought I'd see. What a shame."

"He's an island institution, all right," she agreed.

"Maybe we should buy it," Grady said. "The bait shop, I mean."

Flash's attention was caught by this, and he swiveled his ears toward the phone conversation. He could hardly imagine anything more wonderful than being able to go to the Shipwreck anytime he wanted, maybe even spending all day there. Of course, now he could go to the maritime museum any time he wanted, and spend all day there, too. It was hard to choose.

Aggie chuckled as she opened the car door for Flash. "Looking for a change of career?"

"Looking for a change of paycheck."

Flash jumped up on his seat, and Aggie hesitated, wondering if she should bring up her conversation with Bishop that morning. As she was debating, the door to the hardware store opened and Donny Keller stepped out, raising his arm to her. "Hey, Chief!"

Aggie said, "Gotta go. I've got a copy machine waiting for me to learn how to operate it. Look for my report."

"Love you, babe."

Keller came toward her as she disconnected the call. "I found something else missing," he said gruffly. "A shovel. I had six, now I have five."

Aggie remembered the jumble of merchandise among the broken cement bags and overturned wheelbarrows. "You're sure?"

"I said it, didn't I?" His tone was belligerent as he gestured back toward the store. "Come see for yourself."

"I meant," Aggie replied patiently, "are you sure your inventory is right? Maybe you sold one and didn't record it."

He glared at her. "You saying I don't know my own business? I had six, now I have five. I'm reporting it stolen. You gonna do anything about it or not?"

Aggie said, "All right, Mr. Keller. I'll put it in my report. One shovel, stolen."

She closed the passenger door and walked around the car to get in.

"I want a copy of that report," Keller called after her as she opened the car door.

"You'll get one," she assured him, getting into the vehicle, "certified mail. Have a good day, Mr. Keller."

He muttered, "Good day, my…"

But she closed the door on the rest of the sentence, glancing at Flash as she started the engine. "A shovel," she said. "Forty thousand dollars' worth of merchandise waiting to be stolen, and the man steals a shovel. Go figure."

That sounded to Flash like another one of those "why" questions it was best to save for later pondering. At any rate, there was no time to figure it out now, because as Aggie was turning out of the parking lot, the radio crackled with Sally Ann's voice. "We have a report of a disturbance at Beachside Park, possible assault. Is anyone available?"

Mo's voice came through. "Unit Two, responding. Six minutes."

Aggie pushed the button on her radio. "Unit One, on my way."

Flash dug in his claws and held on, panting with excitement, as Aggie hit the siren and swung out onto Island Road. Mondays. They were his favorite day of the week.

CHAPTER TEN

Beachside Park was located in the center of the island, literally two blocks from the rambling cedar house Aggie shared with Flash and Grady. The park boasted a pavilion big enough for community events, like Aggie and Ryan Grady's wedding, and there were picnic tables scattered across the lawn that overlooked the ocean. Flash and Aggie often had lunch at one of those tables, and Grady joined them when he was able. There was a boardwalk that led to one of the most pristine white sand beaches in the country; a beach on which Flash and Grady ran every morning, where Bishop cast his line into the surf, and where Aggie and Flash played ball almost every evening. That beach boardwalk was now blocked by a human chain twenty people long, all of them with linked arms and angry faces, alternately chanting "Don't take blood money!" and "Save our Shores!"

Aggie and Flash pulled up approximately thirty seconds before Mo did. Flash, as always, was first on the scene, with Aggie following more cautiously, assessing the situation. There were close to a dozen people being prevented from accessing the beach by the human barricade; some confused, some angry, all of them hot and sweaty and frustrated. There were a couple of mothers with children, some middle-aged beach walkers, some twenty-somethings with paddle boards. There was a family that had hauled a beach cart loaded with chairs, umbrellas, and a day's worth of supplies from who knew how far away, and they were in no mood to be told they couldn't go to the beach. According to the gauge on Aggie's car, the temperature was already 87 degrees and the receding tide meant there was virtually no breeze. Tempers, likewise, were beyond the simmering point and ready to flare. Whenever someone approached the barricade, one of its members would lunge forward and shout something about the dying oceans. It was a street fight waiting to happen.

Aggie said, "Flash," and he looked back.

She jerked her head toward a harried-looking mother trying to control two preschoolers who were on the verge of a tantrum. Red-faced and crying, they screamed, "Why not?" and "I want to go in the water!" When Flash trotted up, they were momentarily distracted, calming down as Flash edged close enough for them to pet. The mother was so relieved she didn't even look around to see where he had come from.

Mo pulled her cruiser up beside Aggie's and got out. She was tapping her baton against her palm as she reached Aggie. "You want me to go crack some heads together?"

"Let's see if we can find a more peaceful way," Aggie suggested.

But she had barely finished speaking before a big man with sunburned shoulders, a prominent paunch, and an angry, sweating face broke forward. "Get the hell out of the way, you bunch of damn hippies!" He marched straight toward the human barricade, waving his fist. "You don't own this beach!"

Aggie murmured, "Or maybe not."

She stepped back and gave the siren on her vehicle a two-second blast while Mo thundered forward, yelling, "Break it up! Step back!" Flash raced ahead of her and slid to a crouch when he reached the red-shouldered man, waiting for his orders. Most of the beachgoers thought twice about charging the barricade when they heard the siren, backing away quickly as Mo plowed to the front. But the angry man pushed forward, knocking one of the girls who blocked the walkway to the ground. Mo grabbed his shoulder and flung him aside like a rag doll.

By this time Aggie had reached the fray. She had her own baton out and used it in a double-handed grip to shove aside people who got in her way as she pushed forward toward the girl who had fallen. She caught Flash's eye and said, "Herd!"

Flash sprang into action, moving in a circle between the unruly beachgoers and the shouting members of the barricade, pushing them back with a hard stare or a sharp bark when they got too close. Once he had seen a member of his species do the same with sheep and concluded that people really weren't that much harder to manage, once you got the technique down. The difference was, of course, that you generally weren't allowed to bite people. Sheep were another matter.

Aggie reached the fallen girl, who was being helped to her feet by her comrades. Mo had the assailant sitting on the ground and held him there with her baton pressed hard into his sternum. He was still shouting, "I've got a right! We've all got rights!"

To which Mo replied darkly, "You shut your mouth right now or I'll be reading you your rights." She jabbed the baton harder against his sternum. "And I mean *right now*."

Aggie said to the girl, "Are you hurt? Do you need medical assistance?"

The girl cried, "That's assault! You saw it, Officer! He hit me!"

The man shouted back. "I didn't hit you! But it wasn't because I didn't want to!"

Mo growled at him, "I ain't telling you again."

The girl's friends began to jostle and shout at Aggie. "Arrest him! That's battery! We have a lawful right to assembly!" and, bizarrely, "Defund the police!"

Flash gave a final warning look to one of the beachgoers who started to shout back at the protestors, then whipped around and went to Aggie's side. He fixed some of the more aggressive ones with a stare, and they backed off a little. The others waved their fists at Aggie and continued to shout.

Aggie stood between the two groups, raised her

palms in a firm staying gesture, and said loudly, "Enough! Everybody, quiet! Quiet down right now or I'm going to arrest every one of you and nobody's going to the beach!"

Flash punctuated her words by dropping into his crouch with a low growl and Mo strode forward, eyes churning, baton swinging. The clamor began to die down.

Aggie spotted a boy she knew in the line with the protestors, which dispelled Grady's observation that none of them were local. "Toby Workman, what's the matter with you?" she demanded. "Don't you have anything better to do than hang around with this rabble?"

He didn't look in the least abashed. "We have a right to protest!"

"What are you protesting, exactly?" she shot back.

And without waiting for an answer she swung on the assailant, who was struggling to get up from the grass where Mo had left him. "Mr. Farnsworth, you ought to be ashamed of yourself! You don't go around pushing women down, I don't care how mad you get!"

She turned back to the young woman who had been pushed. "Do you want to press charges?"

The girl looked uneasy, glancing at her colleagues for the answer, and finally landing her gaze on someone beyond Aggie's shoulder. She seemed to find her answer there, and replied in a disgruntled tone, "No. I guess not."

"Then move along," Aggie said crisply. "All of you." The rumblings of discontent began again, and

Aggie raised her voice. "You are blocking a public thoroughfare and I'm calling upon you to disperse. Do it now!"

Mo moved toward them, raising her baton to waist level. "You heard the chief! *Move!*"

Aggie strode over to Mr. Farnsworth, who had finally regained his feet. "You," she told him sharply, "count yourself lucky you're not in jail right now. Go home and cool off."

"But," he started to sputter, "it wasn't my fault! All I did was—"

Aggie reached for her cuffs, and he threw up his hands, backing away and muttering loudly, "Some police service we got around here!"

When she turned, a lanky young man stood there, looking completely unruffled and infuriatingly amused. He was mildly sunburned, like the others in his group, wearing a baseball cap and jeans with a faded navy tee shirt. The shirt had a depiction of a funnel cloud on it, and in Gothic letters, the caption "I Am The Storm." He also had a folded paper in his hand. Aggie knew without asking that he was the leader of the group, the one from whom everyone else took their orders.

He said, "We do have the right to assemble, you know." He handed her the folded paper. "And permits."

Aggie did not have to read the paper to know it was a permit issued by her office for a public event. Nonetheless, she studied it, then looked up. "Are you Cade Rodan?"

"Yes, ma'am," he replied easily. His smile would

have charmed a woman ten years younger than Aggie, and with half her experience.

Aggie refolded the paper and returned it to him. "This permit does not give you the right to create a public disruption or block a public right-of-way. Kindly tell your people to back off. I can promise you they do *not* want to go up against my officer." She glanced over to where Mo, amidst cries of "Police brutality!" was still shoving her baton against people who gave her an argument, and Flash was still threatening to lunge at anyone who talked back. She added meaningfully, "Either of them."

He replied pleasantly, "You know, the right to peaceful protest goes back to the beginnings of this nation. Remember the Boston Tea Party? How about Carrie Nation, or the Suffragettes? And we won't even talk about the Vietnam War. Protest is how this country experiences change, Chief. And the change is almost always for the better."

She looked at him steadily. "You have a valid point. But neither Carrie Nation nor Jane Fonda nor any of those fine people at the Boston Tea Party are giving me a headache right now. You are. So how about you call your people off before I'm forced to do something both of us will regret?"

He looked at her for another moment, that smile on his face slowly beginning to morph into something closely resembling a smirk. Then he turned back toward the beach and called, "Yo, people! Take five!"

Almost just like that, the protestors lost their steam, began to disassemble, and moved away, clearing the beach access. Aggie turned to the frustrated, hot, and confused group of beachgoers who were lined up in front of the walkway. She called, "Okay, folks! Everything is under control. Hit the water and enjoy your day!"

She looked back at Cade. "And I hope I don't have to tell you if you ever try anything like this again, I'm going to throw you and your crew under the jail."

He replied with that same easy smile, "Chief, my father's a cop and my uncle's a lawyer. I know exactly how far I can go."

This irritated Aggie far more than it should have. "They must be so proud," she said.

Flash, pleased with a job well done, returned to Aggie. His ears pricked forward as he got closer to the man she was talking to, and he quickened his pace, interested.

Flash would be the first to admit he did not know everything about this job. Sometimes he made mistakes. He was quick to leap into action, but sometimes it was the wrong action. He was also quick to gather information and come to a conclusion, which was a good thing—except when it wasn't. Aggie, on the other hand, knew everything there was to know about this job, and she almost never made mistakes. He had learned that it was best to take his cues from her.

Except one time there had been a man with a skeleton tattoo on his arm who was some place he should not have been. Flash knew about it, and Aggie didn't. What had happened afterwards had been very bad indeed. Flash did not want to make that mistake again.

Aggie watched as Flash came up and started to sniff Cade's sneakers. Cade glanced down at him, half smiled, and remarked, "Cute dog." He started to turn away. Aggie stopped him.

"Where are you all staying?" she asked.

"The campground at the other end of the island," he replied. "That memorial park donated by Big Oil to make you forget about the hundreds of acres of shoreline that were destroyed, along with the thousands upon thousands of ocean dwelling wildlife."

Flash looked up with interest. He had never heard anything about that. And from the look on Aggie's face, she was having difficulty remembering, too.

"Do you mean Mercury Memorial Park?" she said, frowning a little. "That oil spill was back in the eighties. Mercury Oil isn't even in business anymore."

He smiled complacently. "Oh, yes, it is. Just under another name. And in three years you'll be looking at another one of their offshore drilling rigs, this one with even fewer safety measures than the last one had, thanks to the new and improved EPA. That is unless the citizens of the Gulf Coast band together to make their voices heard."

He reached into his back pocket and brought out a folded flyer, handing it to her. "That's what this so-called environmental center they're putting up in the middle of the park is all about—blood money paid to the people of Dogleg Island to prove what good

DONNA BALL

corporate citizens they are while they're out there poisoning your oceans and destroying your beaches. You want to learn more about what the future really holds for this island, we're having a rally tomorrow during the grand opening. All perfectly permitted, of course," he added with a mockingly raised eyebrow. "Feel free to stop by."

Aggie stuffed the flyer in her pocket without looking at it while a trickle of sweat escaped her cap and dripped past her ear. She was ready to get back inside her air-conditioned vehicle. "Look," she said, "you're welcome to march around in the heat and chant and hand out literature all you want. But this is your last warning about harassing the public. I expect you to stay behind the barriers and away from the building during the grand opening tomorrow. Any disruption of the ceremony will be considered a violation of your permit. And stay hydrated," she added with an impatient frown as Mo walked up. "I don't want my next call out here to be with an ambulance."

He grinned and touched a finger to the brim of his ball cap as he walked away.

"You were mighty nice to that troublemaker," Mo grumbled, scowling after him. Her face was shiny with sweat, her hands resting on her gun belt in a way that suggested she was ready to respond to even the slightest provocation.

Aggie sighed and blotted her face. "It's the law, Mo. We can only do what we can do." She glanced at her. "What did you find with the welfare check on Grace

82

Henderson?"

Mo's frown deepened. "Now, that's worrisome. She didn't answer the door, I didn't see a car. The slider was unlocked, so I announced myself and went on in. Everything looked fine, neat as a pin, but no Miz Henderson. I talked to the neighbors on either side and across the street, but nobody remembered seeing her after she left for church Sunday."

Aggie said, "That doesn't sound good. Where does she go to church?"

"First Methodist across the bridge," she replied. "I was getting ready to call the church office, see if they could put me in touch with some of her friends."

Aggie nodded. "Good. Let's make those calls back at the office, what do you say? Flash and I are going to stop for a milkshake, you want anything?"

"Yeah, I wouldn't mind a strawberry with extra whipped cream," Mo agreed, and they walked back to their cars.

"And a vanilla cone for Flash," Aggie said, rubbing his ears.

Flash followed along, relieved now that Aggie had mentioned the law—and the vanilla cone. The law was the one thing that was forever confusing to Flash. The law meant that sometimes you could arrest a bad guy and sometimes you couldn't. The law meant that one fellow might be drinking whiskey in Pete's bar and go home to his wife, while another might drink the same whiskey and go to jail. The law meant some people got to have guns in their cars and others didn't. The law was, to Flash's way of thinking anyway, something best left to Aggie.

And that was probably why she hadn't said anything about the bandage on the back of that man's hand.

CHAPTER ELEVEN

Aggie finished up her cherry-chocolate-chip milkshake at the same time she finished her report on the hardware store break-in. Flash enjoyed his vanilla cone lying on the floor with his paws around his silver bowl, licking up every ounce of the ice cream before starting to crunch up the cone. Aggie pushed "send" on the copy of her report to the sheriff's office and was about to start filling out the report on the incident at the park when Sally Ann tapped timidly on the doorframe.

"Excuse me, Chief. Is this a good time?"

It was not a good time. It would never be a good time for what Aggie knew Sally Ann had to say. Nonetheless she smiled and beckoned her in. "Sure," she said, tossing her empty milkshake cup into the trash. "Have a seat. Isn't this space amazing, Sally Ann?" she went on, not in the least embarrassed to sink to the level of trying to distract Sally Ann from the purpose of her visit. "No comparison to what we're used to, huh? Don't you love it? I hear we even have a new copy machine."

"Yes, ma'am." Sally Ann brought one of the straight chairs from the corner and sat down in front of Aggie's desk. Her expression was resolute, and, despite the pigtails and flowered skirt that made her look half her twenty-three years, Aggie found herself intimidated.

"Chief," Sally Ann said firmly, "I gave you almost three months' notice. I said I'd stay and help you get moved into the new office, and I have. But classes start the twenty-eighth, and that gives me less than a week to train my replacement—which you haven't even hired yet."

Aggie sighed. Sally Ann Mitchell, bright, eager, and far too young to be as good at her job as she was, had managed the Dogleg Island Police Station since its inception. She took calls, dispatched emergencies, kept the logs, filed reports, managed payroll, and did a dozen other jobs that Aggie herself barely understood, all on a salary that scarcely exceeded minimum wage. Aggie, Sally Ann, and Mo had started together on the first day the Dogleg Island Police Department opened its doors and somehow, in her mind, Aggie had always pictured them staying together.

Logically, of course, she knew better. For the past two years, Sally Ann had been taking business classes at night from the community college; now she had decided to transfer to FSU for her degree and work part time at her father's real estate office here on the island. Aggie had tried to talk her into working for the police department part time, instead of for her father, but Sally Ann wasn't interested. She pointed out, rightly, that hers was not a part-time job, but Aggie knew that was not entirely the reason. Sally Ann had been there when a squadron of vigilantes sprayed automatic gunfire throughout this very building, and she had watched a young man on whom she had a crush die. Aggie suspected that police work, at that moment, had become a little too real for the young woman. Leaving was the best thing for her. But it was not the best thing for Aggie.

"I know," Aggie apologized, "and I'm sorry. It's been a little hectic around here, you know, and to tell the truth, I just haven't found the right candidate."

Flash had to agree with that. The first person to come in was Colonel Bowes, retired from the Marines and a volunteer fireman who was looking to get a toehold in law enforcement even though he was too old for the Academy. He was nice enough and told lots of interesting stories, but he typed with one finger on the computer and accidentally wiped out a whole week's work of Sally Ann's reports. Besides, what was he going to do if there was a fire? Likewise, there was the woman from Ocean City, who smelled like sour milk and who talked far too much about how much trouble she had had giving birth to her two children. Flash could see Aggie's face losing color with every word.

"What about Mackenzie?" Sally Ann pressed.

The applicant to whom she referred was a friend of Sally Ann's from night school who had the necessary secretarial skills, but little else.

Aggie shook her head, her expression dry. "I cannot hire a person who posts a picture of herself on social media with a bunch of frat boys doing Jello shots out of her navel."

"Oh." Sally Ann looked taken aback. Clearly, she didn't know her friend as well as she thought she did. "Well, what about that woman who was in last week? Her resume was good."

Again Aggie shook her head. "She needed Wednesdays and Fridays off during the summer. Childcare problems." Not to mention the fact that she had spent the entire interview sniffing into a tissue. With four elementary-school-aged children, the woman was a walking germ factory.

"Well, what about…"

"He had a criminal record!" objected Aggie, knowing exactly which blond surfer-dude Sally Ann was referring to.

"Just shoplifting," Sally Ann pointed out a little testily.

Aggie sighed. "Look, Sally Ann, I'm doing my best. But this is a sensitive job that requires a lot of skill for not much pay, as you know. Not to mention that we don't exactly have a huge labor pool here on the island. Are you sure there isn't some way we can work something out with you? Maybe job-sharing," she suggested hopefully. "If you could work three days and that woman with all the kids could work two…"

Sally Ann shook her head firmly, rising. "You've *got* to find someone, Chief." She started to go, then looked back with her face suddenly filled with remorse.

"Chief, I'm really, really sorry to do this to you with the baby coming and all, but…"

Now it was Aggie who was swamped with guilt. Don't say another word," she said firmly. "I'm the one who's sorry. I've been putting this off because I don't want you to leave, and that's silly of me. I *want* you to get your degree. Of course I do." She smiled. "And then I want you to come back here and run this police station even better than you do now."

Aggie drew a breath. "So how about this? I've got an ad in the paper this week. We're bound to get lots of applicants. You screen them, put them through their paces, find the one you think is most qualified, and then bring them to me. Barring a criminal record or gross incompetence, I'll approve your choice. Scout's honor."

Sally Ann's shoulders sagged with relief. She said, "Thanks, Chief."

But Flash could see a bright film of tears pop into Sally Ann's eyes, and he didn't want her to feel bad, so he came to stand beside her, leaning a comforting shoulder against her leg. For some reason, this seemed to make her feel worse, and she ducked her head to pet him, trying to hide the tears. "I'm going to miss you, Flash," she said thickly. She looked as though she wanted to say more, but the phone in the outer office started to ring, and she hurried to answer it.

Flash went back to Aggie, who looked as unhappy as Sally Ann had been. She dropped her hand to Flash's head with a sigh. "I know things have to change, Flash," she said. "But why does everything have to change at once?"

He had no answer for that.

Mo tapped on Aggie's doorframe. "I'm not having much luck with Miz Henderson," she said, "and her daughter just called again. I told her not to worry and we were still looking, and like as not her mother had just decided to go on an overnight and forgot to tell anybody."

Aggie suggested, "Maybe she has a boyfriend."

Mo consulted her notebook. "Not according to anybody I talked to. She has book club second Tuesday night of the month, Bible study every other Wednesday, volunteers at the library on Fridays. She runs the historical society with Miz Billings, but it's only open Tuesday through Friday. Nobody I talked to knew anything about her planning to go out of town. Sheriff's office didn't have any accident or breakdown reports involving her vehicle."

Aggie said, "Did you check the hospital?"

She nodded. "Nothing."

Aggie stood. "Okay, text me the tag number and description of her vehicle. Let's take a turn around the island and see if we can spot it. It's too early to declare her a missing person, but in this heat, at her age, we can't be too careful."

"Yes, sir." Mo flipped her notebook shut. "You go east, I go west?"

"Sounds like a plan."

Flash loved going on patrol, particularly when he could ride with the window open and the smell of the ocean blowing through his fur. Aggie said it was too hot to do that now, but still, there was nothing better than sitting tall in his seat, keeping an eye out for things, while the streets of Dogleg Island rolled by.

He raced to their vehicle as soon as Aggie opened the door, but was struck by disappointment when Aggie, instead of following him to the SUV, started walking in the opposite direction, down the shell path that led toward the community garden. The disappointment vanished when Flash saw where she was going, and he dashed ahead to greet the gardener.

Flash liked just about everybody, but Mason McMasters was without a doubt one of the most interesting people he'd ever met. He knew how to make water out of air and food out of dirt. He had a spaceship with flames coming out of it painted on his truck. Once Flash had listened to him explain to a group of schoolchildren how a tiny seed no bigger than a grain of sand could make a whole tomato vine with dozens of tomatoes on it that you could actually eat, which sounded like magic to Flash. He wouldn't have believed it if he hadn't seen it with his own eyes by virtue of checking, every single day, the ground where the seeds were planted until, yes, actual vines started climbing toward the sky. Of course, the question of why anyone would *want* a tomato vine with dozens of tomatoes on it remained a mystery, but that did not take away from the magnificence of Mr. McMasters as far as Flash was concerned.

Mason McMasters, dressed in dirty khakis, a long-sleeved shirt open over a tee shirt, and a wide-brimmed hat, was chuckling and giving Flash a full-body rubdown when Aggie arrived. "Mr. McMasters," she scolded mildly, squinting in the sun. "I would think that you of all people would know better. It's almost ninety degrees out here."

He was not a young man; Aggie guessed early seventies or late sixties, but he was wiry and fit, leather-skinned, and easy-going. He was something of recluse, living in a cottage on the leeward side of the island that he had built himself, surrounded by two acres of cultivated tropical gardens and hoop houses. Aggie had been there once with Lorraine when she went in search of Asian lilies for the decorative flowerpots around her pool. Although McMasters did not advertise a retail business, Lorraine confided to Aggie that everyone who cared anything about gardening knew he was the person to go to for the best plants. When they visited, he had had hundreds of the most beautiful lilies Aggie had ever seen, in all different colors and hues. Lorraine had bought a dozen, and even Aggie, who considered herself the resigned owner of a brown thumb, couldn't resist investing in a ruby-red lily for the flower bed in front of their house. It grew almost five feet tall and bloomed every spring to this day.

He grinned up at her, tilting back his sweat-stained hat. "Yes, ma'am, Miss Chief," he said. "I'm just about to call it a day." He straightened up, and she saw he was wearing a canvas harvest bag across his body. "The Garrisons had to head north for the season, and I hated to see all this zucchini go to waste. Thought I'd donate it to the food bank."

The community garden was divided into eighteen 6X8 raised-bed plots which members of the community could lease for $25. 00 a year—roughly the cost of water. There had been so much interest when the project was first announced that applicants had been chosen via lottery. Aggie and Grady, who had much more pressing matters to deal with at the time, had not submitted an application. Thinking about another mouth to feed next year—one who would certainly benefit from organic vegetables—Aggie thought it might not be a bad idea to throw her name into the hat for a plot next year.

Aggie said, "You should have been at the party this morning. Jess from the paper was there taking pictures, and since you're the one who donated all the landscaping to the community center, it doesn't seem right that you weren't in the photos."

He shook his head modestly. "Nah, I never was much for getting my picture taken. Who wants to look at an ugly old cuss like me, anyway?"

Aggie gave him a look of mock reprimand. "Well, we're having a grand opening for the public soon, and we'll all be hurt if you're not there, pictures or no pictures."

She glanced around the spent garden. The growing season in this part of the Panhandle was roughly February through June—with the exception of outliers like zucchini, peppers, cucumbers, and melons—and most of the plots had either been stripped, or were sporting bare, withered yellow and brown plants long past their prime. There was a pile of debris waist-high in one corner of the lot where gardeners had cleared their plots of spent plants and vines. Aggie nodded toward the pile and reminded McMasters, "The county still isn't issuing burn permits."

"Yes'm, I know. I'm thinking about building a compost box, and what's not compostable, we'll mulch."

Aggie tilted back her cap to wipe the sweat from her hairline. "That's very ecologically minded of you, Mr. McMasters."

"I figured it's the least we can do, given as how Mother Nature is already so pissed at us."

Aggie smiled. "So *that's* what this drought is all about."

He replied seriously, "The temperature of the ocean is close to 92 degrees. Coral reefs are dying. Fish are smothering. Pretty soon they'll be boiling."

Flash looked at him in alarm. He had noticed that playing in the surf was not nearly as refreshing as it once had been, and that running along the tideline never cooled his paws. But fish, boiling? Could that be true?

McMasters went on, "We're in for a hell of a hurricane season, Chief. Maybe not this year, but surely next. And these barrier islands—Dogleg, Wild Horse, Siesta, Jupiter, all the islands down the Florida coast—they're what protect the mainland. When they're gone, there's nothing between the continent and a natural disaster."

Flash looked to Aggie for reassurance, trying to get the picture of boiling fish out of his head. She did not look very reassuring. In fact, she looked as troubled as he was.

Aggie murmured weakly, "I'm so glad I stopped by."

She started to bid him good day, then paused. "Say, Mr. McMasters, you were here during the Mercury oil spill, weren't you?"

He wiped his face with the already-sweat-stained bandanna he wore around his neck. "Nineteen eighty-three," he replied. "Now, that was a mess if ever there was one. Dead fish washing up on the beach every day, big dolphins, sea turtles too. You couldn't walk barefoot on the beach for getting your feet stained with tar. Couldn't wear your shoes in the house for tracking it in. It took them over a year to get it cleaned up. Then, when they started building the park, even more trouble. Brought the military in to close down site eventually."

"The military?" Aggie said, surprised. "What on earth for?"

He shrugged. "Oh, there were all kinds of rumors floating around, if I recall. Everything from an alien spaceship to radioactive trash. They even tried to get me to evacuate while they cleaned up whatever it was, being so close to the site like I was, but where was I supposed to go?" He shrugged. "I don't think anybody ever knew for sure what it was all about. Myself, I live mostly off the grid, and that's why. The less I know about things like that, the better off I am."

"I guess," Aggie agreed absently, wondering if even

Grady knew the story behind the building of the park. "It was nice talking to you, Mr. McMasters." She added, "But let's all get out of the sun. You take care, now."

At the car, she took two bottles of water out of the cooler in the back. She poured one into Flash's bowl and had just finished drinking her own when the radio call from Mo came in.

"Chief," she said, "I spotted Miz Henderson's car in front of the Historical Society. The place is locked up and nobody answers my knock, but I looked in the window and saw a woman's purse on the front desk. What do you want to do?"

Flash took a final slurp of his water and jumped into the passenger seat of the waiting vehicle. Aggie emptied his bowl on the ground and went around to the driver's side. "Call Mrs. Billings and see if she can bring you a key. Try calling the number of the office. Maybe Mrs. Henderson is working in back and can't hear you knocking. I'm two minutes out."

Flash dug in his claws as Aggie spun out of the parking lot. They were on the job again, and there was no time to waste.

CHAPTER
TWELVE

The Historical Society was housed in a small metal building in the middle of a crushed shell parking lot. There were no other structures on the short sand road, and no one to tell them if Grace Henderson had entered the building, or when. Heat rose up from the white shell lot in waves, burning Flash's paws as he hopped out of the vehicle and began his perimeter search of the building. Mo came forward when Aggie got out, looking hot and worried.

"Miz Billings is on her way over," she reported. "Said it'd be fifteen or twenty minutes. I've been letting the phone ring inside. I can hear it from out here. I don't know why anybody inside wouldn't."

Aggie looked in the window next to the door, cupping her hands around her eyes to cut the glare. The reception room was just big enough to accommodate a desk and a couple of chairs, and in the gloomy interior Aggie could see the woman's purse, white leather with a shoulder strap, lying atop the desk as Mo had described.

"The lights aren't on," Aggie observed, stepping away. "She might have forgotten her purse."

"I checked the car," Mo added. "It's locked, too. Maybe it wouldn't start and she walked to town to try to call for help."

"Maybe," Aggie agreed uncertainly, looking around.

But Flash knew otherwise. Part of his job—maybe the most important part—was noticing things with his nose that Aggie had yet to notice with her eyes. Sometimes these things were good. Sometimes they were not. Flash had not even made a full circuit around the building before he realized that what was inside was not good.

Aggie started to walk around the building, looking for another point of entrance, when Flash intercepted her. He flung himself on the front door and clawed at the handle, which didn't budge.

Aggie barely wasted a moment. She said sharply to Mo, "Break the lock!"

Flash moved to the window and threw his paws against it. He knew what was inside, and there was no time to be subtle. He spun back to the door.

Mo returned from her vehicle with a short, heavy tool. She commanded Flash, "Back off!" and she thrust the tool against the door once, twice before the lock cracked and the door sprang open. Flash rushed inside.

Aggie gasped as the hot air inside the building hit her like a wall. "Jesus, Mo," she managed, stumbling inside, "it's got to be a hundred and twenty in here! Why is there no air-conditioning?"

Flash was already behind the desk, having found what he was looking for. Aggie fell to her knees beside him, and for a moment she couldn't speak.

Grace Henderson lay there, her hands and feet bound with clear shipping tape, her mouth wrapped in layers of the same tape. She was white-faced, still, unmoving.

"Holy God," Mo whispered at Aggie's shoulder.

"Get an ambulance!" Aggie said, tugging at the tape across the woman's mouth.

Mo was already dialing. Flash backed off, panting rapidly, watching from a corner and making himself small. This was the part he didn't like.

Mo found scissors in the desk and cut the tape from the woman's hands and ankles while Aggie tugged the tape from her mouth and quickly checked her pulse and breath sounds. "She's still breathing," Aggie gasped. "I've barely got a pulse." She wiped the sweat out of her eyes with the back of her arm. "We need to get her out of here. Then find some wet towels. She's burning up."

Mo got to her feet. "I've got ice in the cooler."

"No, it might put her into shock." Aggie looked around frantically and spotted the air-conditioning unit in the window. "See if that thing is working. I'll look for a restroom."

DONNA BALL

Flash saw the door on the back wall and ran to it, slapping the doorknob with his paws. Mo reached it before Aggie could and swung it open. "Air-conditioning!" she called.

Mo dragged the woman across the threshold into what appeared to be a vast, shockingly cool, storage space filled with shelves of books and boxes. Some of those boxes were overturned, their contents spilling onto the floor; others had been dumped onto one of the two long, library-type tables that formed an L in the center of the room. Aggie barely noticed the disarray as she and Mo took turns running back and forth to the small lavatory, soaking paper towels in cool water and returning to cover the victim with them. Flash waited outside until the ambulance came. Watching Aggie and Mo work so hard to try to save the burning-up woman just made him sad.

Nora Billings arrived with the key to the building just as the EMTs were loading Grace Henderson into the ambulance. She looked distraught as her gaze swiveled from Aggie to the ambulance, clutching her keys helplessly. "My God!" she exclaimed. "What happened? Is that—is that Grace?" She started toward the ambulance, but the doors were already closed. She turned to Aggie. "Was that Grace Henderson? What happened?"

Aggie finished pouring a bottle of water into Flash's bowl and drank half a bottle herself before answering. "We're hoping you can help us answer that, Mrs. Billings," she said. She dug into the cooler of half-melted ice and splashed icy water on her wrists and neck. "We found Mrs. Henderson inside the building, bound and gagged," she explained. "No one had seen or heard from her since yesterday morning, and we're afraid she might have been there for almost twenty-four hours. Why is there no air-conditioning in the office?"

"Oh!" gasped Nora, sinking back against her car door. She was a thin, middle-aged woman with a severe black haircut and rimless glasses. Behind those glasses her eyes were huge with shock. "Oh, my goodness! Is she... will she be okay?"

Aggie soaked a paper towel in ice water and draped it around Flash's neck while he lapped up the water in his bowl. "I don't know," she said. "She was unconscious. The EMTs said it looked like heat stroke."

While Nora took a moment to absorb this, Aggie finished her bottle of water and uncapped another. Mo, standing by her own vehicle, poured a bottle of water over her head, shook out her tight dark curls, and splashed ice water from her cooler over her face and arms. She came to join them as the ambulance pulled away with Grace Henderson inside.

Aggie said to Nora, "Do you have any idea what Grace Henderson might have been doing here?"

Nora started to shake her head, then said uncertainly, "She was writing an article for the paper about the first school on Dogleg Island. You know, that column they do sometimes called 'Back in the Day'? She might have needed some photographs or something."

Mo said, "Any notion about who would want to

hurt her? Somebody that might've followed her here, maybe?"

Nora shook her head adamantly this time. "Sweet Grace? She didn't have an enemy in the world. I just can't imagine something like this happening, here of all places!"

Aggie gestured toward the building. "Could you come inside and look around? Tell us if anything is missing or out of place."

"And why wasn't the damn air-conditioning on?" Mo demanded, following them inside.

Nora fluttered a hand to her throat as they entered the building. "Oh, we don't air-condition the office when we're not here." She went quickly to turn on the window unit. "We have to keep the documents room cool all the time, of course."

"So," Aggie speculated, looking around. "She came in the front door, locked it behind her, put her purse on the desk, and either didn't have time to turn on the lights and AC, or didn't think she'd be in the office long enough to need them."

"Is there another way in?" Mo asked.

"There's a back door," replied Nora, leading the way through the open door to the document room, "but the lock sticks and we never use it. Besides, nobody wants to park by the trash cans."

Flash was already trotting toward the back door, which he had discovered while waiting for the ambulance. Mo said, "I'll check it out." And followed him.

"Oh, my word." Nora stopped short as she

surveyed the chaos of overturned boxes and spilled papers in the room. "What happened here?"

She started forward toward the long table, as though to clean up the mess, but Aggie blocked her with an outstretched arm. "What do you keep in here?"

"Oh," she said weakly, eyes scanning the disordered room with increasing dismay, "all sorts of things. Photographs, drawings, maps, surveys, old newspaper clippings, diaries... the kinds of things people turn over from their relatives' estates, you know, birth certificates, death certificates, books on genealogy, island records, ledger books..." She exhaled a huge breath. "Oh, my. It really is a mess, isn't it?"

"What are people usually looking for when they come here?" Aggie asked.

Nora blinked several times, seeming to gather her thoughts. "Oh. Um, well, it's mostly people trying to trace their ancestry, put together a family tree, you know. There's a genealogical society in Ocean City; they come here a lot."

"Do you keep any valuables here? Antiques or artifacts or anything like that?"

"Oh, dear, no," replied Nora, looking mildly alarmed. "Anything that we receive like that goes straight to the museum. We really can't afford the insurance," she confided, "or the security."

Aggie asked, "Can you think of any reason why someone would want to break in here?"

She looked completely baffled. "None. We're open to the public. There's no charge for anything. All you have to do is come in during business hours."

That was the second time Aggie had heard that today.

From the back of the room, Mo called, "Yo, Chief! You'll want to look at this."

Aggie told Nora, "Don't touch anything just yet. I'll be back."

Aggie found Flash and Mo at the back of the building where a short corridor led to a plain wooden door, now standing open. The simple thumb-turn lock had been jimmied in much the same way as the one in the records office, although this one—as evidenced by the bent faceplate—had obviously required a bit more force. Aggie examined the damage briefly, took some pictures, and looked around the area for additional evidence, although she knew if there was any, Flash already would have found it. She came to stand beside Mo again, and the two women were silent for a moment.

Aggie said, "Are you thinking what I'm thinking?"

Mo answered, "That we've had more break-ins in one morning than we've had all summer?"

"So what's changed?"

Mo was quick to respond. "A bunch of hippie no-good troublemakers marching around Beachside Park."

Aggie frowned. "And what *are* they protesting against, anyway?"

"I say nothing," Mo responded. "I say it's just a cover for a crime spree."

Aggie's brow twisted with frustration. "But it's

stupid. Nothing of value was taken, not here, not at the records office this morning—both places you can just walk into and find whatever you want for free. It makes no sense."

"Mischief don't need a reason," Mo insisted.

After a moment, Aggie sighed. "All right, let's do an ID check on every one of those beach bums. If anybody gives you any backtalk, bring him in, and by that, I mean in particular the leader, Mr. My-Dad-Is-A-Cop-And-My-Uncle-Is-A-Lawyer."

"Yes, sir, on it." Despite the stresses of the past half hour, Mo's lips twitched with pleasure. "You need any help here?"

"No," Aggie said. "I'll get whatever prints I can and photograph the scene. You go on. I'll meet you back at the office."

Aggie spent the next forty-five minutes processing the scene, although she had little hope that any of her documentation would lead to a suspect. The crime still seemed senseless. Aggie had examined Grace's purse before the EMTs took her away, and she found a wallet with credit cards, ID, and almost $200 in cash, all intact. Even her phone was undisturbed. Robbery did not appear to be the motive unless the thief had taken something from the building that Nora had yet to identify.

Aggie found Nora on the phone when she and Flash returned to the front office, which by now had been cooled by the window unit to a bearable temperature. "I was just letting some of her friends know what happened," Nora said when she disconnected. "A bunch of us are going down to the hospital to be with her. She has a daughter in Ohio, I think, but I don't have a number."

Aggie said, "I'll take care of it. But it's really important that you go through those spilled papers and see if anything is missing. Do you keep a master list or catalog?"

She looked mildly insulted. "Of course. That's what we *do*. We catalog items of historical interest."

"So if you could check the papers against the catalog and let me know if anything is missing, it might help us figure out who did this, and why."

Her lips tightened with resolve. "I'll get some volunteers in here right away."

Aggie and Flash went back to the unit and Aggie turned the AC up full blast, sitting there for a moment while the vehicle cooled down. She was not looking forward to making that call to Grace Henderson's daughter. Meanwhile, there were four or five other elderly residents that she needed to check on. And she was starving.

"You know, Flash," she said as she put the vehicle in gear, "usually when you see a pattern like this, there's an obvious connection between the crimes. But I swear I can't see it. And why would you go to all the trouble to tie up an elderly woman and leave her to suffocate, then not steal anything?"

That was another one of those questions for which Flash had no answer, but then the vagaries of human behavior always baffled him. Why did Mr. Keller steal things from his own store? Why did people give Mr.

Obediah money for crabs in a wire cage when they could pick them up for free on the beach? Why did Margaret Dillon keep fish in a glass box in her office, and why would anyone want to hurt a nice lady like Mrs. Henderson? It was all a mystery.

But he could rest easy knowing that even though there were multiple things in this world he didn't understand, Aggie would have no trouble at all figuring them out.

CHAPTER THIRTEEN

Pete's Place Bar and Grille was one of the most iconic places on Dogleg, and up until The Bistro Fine Dining had opened up downtown, it was the only full-service restaurant on the island. Everyone, from construction workers to bankers to tourists, eventually found their way to Pete's. The reason, as far as Flash was concerned, was simple: nobody knew how to make a hamburger like Pete.

Aggie and Flash hardly ever had time during the week to have lunch at Pete's, but Grady had texted he was on his way across the bridge to deliver a subpoena and wanted to meet for a quick lunch. That was fine with Aggie, and more than fine with Flash.

It was late for the working crowd, who started their days at dawn and took their lunch breaks at 11:00, and early for the across-the-bridge folks, who liked to drift over to the island between 2:00 and 3:00

for an afternoon of shopping and beach-going that usually ended in a cocktail and an early supper before heading home. Most of the tables were finishing up, and only one or two people were at the bar. Aggie and Flash paused a moment to glance around, noting the familiar faces of the summer people even if they didn't know all their names. A few faces they didn't recognize at all, but it was always that way at Pete's.

The walls were rough planked and decorated with ship's wheels and fish nets and vintage photographs of the Dogleg Island of yesteryear. The rich aroma of frying foods and spilled beer that had occasionally made Aggie nauseous of late now just made her hungry. Bob Segar was on the speakers and Pete was behind the glossy mahogany bar. He raised a finger to them in acknowledgement as they came in.

Flash, having checked out the occupants of the room and greeted the ones he was friendly with, trotted to his stool at the end of the bar and hopped up on it. This never failed to make someone laugh, and others wanted to take pictures with their phones. Flash was used to it, and always made sure to smile.

Aggie slid onto the stool next to him, and Pete said, "The usual?"

Aggie held up two fingers. "Make it a double."

Pete lifted an eyebrow as he turned to the built-in cooler and poured a glass of milk. "Rough day?" He added two scoops of vanilla ice cream and a straw and brought it to her.

She answered wearily, "It's only been one day?" She stirred the ice cream into the milk and took a sip, closing her eyes in utter contentment. "This hits the spot."

Pete filled a bowl with ice and water and set it before Flash. "I heard you had some trouble at Beachside Park this morning."

She shrugged. "Nothing Mo and I couldn't handle."

"A group of those rowdys were in here Saturday night, passing out leaflets and trying to preach a sermon. I finally had to threaten to throw them out if they didn't stop bothering my customers."

Aggie said, "Yeah, looks like they're trying to get some kind of recruitment campaign going, although for what I still don't know."

"That's all this island needs," Pete said. "A bunch of outside agitators coming in trying to stir up trouble over nothing." He nodded at the glass in Aggie's hand. "How about a little protein to go with that?"

"Yeah, okay." She glanced around. "Ryan is on his way. Is the patio closed?"

"Excessive heat warning," he explained. "Against health code."

Aggie slid a glance toward Flash, her expression dry. "So is serving canines at the bar, but that never bothered you."

Flash looked up from lapping up his ice water, but Pete just grinned, taking out his order pad. "Let me get your order in. How about a couple of captain's platters?"

Aggie shook her head regretfully. "We both have to get back to work. Let's make it two chicken salad sandwiches with extra fries."

He made a face. "Bad choice. Lorraine didn't get a chance to make the chicken salad before she left to pick up Gabby from school, and the way Luis makes it is too spicey for you."

Gabby was Pete and Lorraine's six-year-old foster daughter, soon to be an official and permanent member of the family. She had come to them deaf and mostly nonverbal but was making remarkable progress in the special education classes she attended five hours a day. Lorraine had found a new lease on life since it had begun to revolve around Gabby, and Aggie, for the first time, understood how she felt.

Pete said, "I got some nice flounder in this morning."

"Grill it up and put it in two buns, and you've got a deal. No coleslaw, extra fries."

Pete made a note, and Flash watched carefully until Pete added, "And a hamburger for Flash." He finished writing and called, "Manny!"

A young Hispanic man pushed through the swinging door to the kitchen carrying a bussing tub. He wore a "Pete's Place is the Place" logo tee shirt and his glossy black hair was tied back at the nape. He grinned when he saw Aggie and Flash. "Hello, Chief Aggie, hello, Flash!" he greeted them. "I get your booth cleared off for you lightning-quick."

Pete held out the ticket to him. "Tell Luis to get started on this order first, will you? The chief is in a hurry."

"Yes, sir, boss." Manny put down the tub and took the ticket, giving Flash's ears a quick rub on his way back to the kitchen.

Aggie smiled as she watched him go. Manny was Gabby's older brother and only living relative. He had been struggling to provide for her when, through a series of twisted events, Pete and Lorraine changed both their lives. Though their relationship had not started out on the best of terms, Pete and Lorraine had taken Manny under their wing when he was released from the hospital after a near-fatal shooting. They found him a place to live and promised him a job at the bar and help obtaining citizenship as long as he stayed in school. So far, the arrangement seemed to be working well, and two months ago Pete and Lorraine had initiated formal proceedings to adopt Gabby. Aggie suspected they would have adopted Manny as well had he not already reached the age of majority.

"Funny how things work out," she said. "To think, the first time you met Manny you were holding him on the floor with a shotgun at his neck."

Pete frowned and pointed out uncomfortably, "After he broke into my house."

Aggie took another sip of her improvised milkshake. "Speaking of break-ins, somebody broke into the historical society building yesterday."

"Jesus." His face twisted with skeptical disdain. "What on earth for?"

"My question exactly. Apparently, Grace Henderson intercepted them. They left her tied up on the floor overnight in an un-air-conditioned room. She's in the hospital now, unconscious."

Pete shook his head slowly, his expression dark.

"Good God, Aggie, what kind of world are we living in?"

She agreed, "That's something I've been asking myself a lot lately."

Her attention was caught by one of the photographs on the wall behind the bar. She must have glanced at it a hundred times but had never really noticed it before. "Say, Pete, can I see that picture behind you? The one with the men in suits and hardhats, standing in front of that sign."

Pete looked over his shoulder, located the framed photograph, and took it off the hanger. He read the label on the back. "Groundbreaking ceremony, Mercury Park, Dogleg Island, 1983." He handed it to her.

Aggie studied the black and white photo with a frown. Four men stood in front of a sign that read, as best as she could make out, *Future Home of Mercury Memorial Park*. All the men wore broad politician's grins, old-fashioned suits, and hard hats. One of them held a shovel.

"Weird," Aggie said. "You know how you can go all your life without hearing a particular word and then you hear it five times in one day? Well, it's been months since I even thought about Mercury Park, and now I hear about it every time I turn around."

Flash's ears pricked up at this. He knew a pattern when he heard one.

Pete said, "Yeah, I think I heard those rabble-rousers talking about holding a rally there. You going?"

Aggie replied, without looking up from the photo, "There will be a strong police presence."

She started to hand the photo back to him, then hesitated. "There's something wrong with this picture," she said, frowning over it again. "This doesn't look like Mercury Park."

"Well, it was forty years and"—Pete counted in his head—"about sixteen hurricanes ago. Things change."

"Yeah, but look at the ground." She pointed. "It's all grass. Mercury Park is beachside."

Pete shrugged and took the photo from her. "What can I tell you? It is what it is."

Aggie glanced around the room as he rehung the picture. "Where did you get all these pictures and things, anyway?"

He turned around. "Here and there. Flea markets, thrift shops, antique stores. Some family stuff, like the ship's wheel and that picture of Dad and Grandad with the bluefin over there, was donated. Lorraine did most of the decorating."

"Nothing from the historical society, then?"

His expression was dry. "I'm not your suspect, Aggie. I have an alibi. Besides, my sister-in-law is a cop."

"So's your brother." Grady came up behind Aggie and touched her shoulder lightly. "What'd he do now?"

Aggie tilted her head back to smile at him, and Flash jumped down from his stool to greet him. "I ordered for you," Aggie said. "Did you get your subpoena served?"

"I did." Grady scratched Flash's chin. "But I've got to be back in forty-five."

Pete set a Coke on a coaster in front of him. "Aggie was just telling me what happened to Grace Henderson."

Aggie and Grady kept in regular touch during the day via text about matters consequential and mundane: who was just arrested on DUI, what to have for dinner, who was involved in a domestic disturbance, whether Aggie thought blue or gray was a better backdrop for the redesigned county website. Bishop often said that their marriage was the best thing that had ever happened to county law enforcement, since everything that happened on either side of the bridge was known to the other office in real time.

Grady said, "Any word?"

Aggie shook her head. "They were treating her in the ER when I left."

Grady picked up his Coke and took a drink. "Did you check out the usual suspects?"

"I would have," replied Aggie unhappily, "but they're all on the other side of the bridge and out of my jurisdiction. I'll submit a formal request to Bishop when I get back to the office."

Grady smiled and held up a collection of folders. "Brought you a present. We checked out as many of the lowlifes as we could. These are the ones without alibis."

Aggie pressed the folders to her chest, beaming. "You are the best husband I ever had," she declared.

"And not a half-bad cop."

"Okay, you lovebirds," Pete said, "your table is ready. Food will be out in a minute."

Grady held up his closed hand for a fist bump. "Thanks, bro. We ought to eat here more often."

They took their drinks to the booth Manny had just cleared and Flash found his place beneath the table, out of the way of passing feet but still allowing him a clear view of everyone who came and went. "So what's the deal?" Aggie said as they slid into opposite sides of the booth. "I've seen more of you today than I did on our last day off. Not that I don't appreciate it," she added, "but the chief deputy doesn't usually deliver subpoenas and you could have texted me these names." She held up the file folders.

Grady let his eyes wander casually toward the door as a couple of diners departed. He said, "I was just wondering how it was going on your first day in the new place."

Aggie lowered her gaze to her glass, stirring the remnants of the almost-melted ice cream with her straw. Of course he would understand. And of course he would be here for her.

"It was a little rough at first," she admitted. She glanced at him. "Flashbacks, you know. To tell the truth, I'm kind of glad all the calls kept me out of the office most of the morning."

Grady nodded. "Yeah, it was the same for me when we first started working there fixing the place up." His restless, sea-watching eyes returned to her, gentle and calm. "It got better with every coat of paint. Margaret

Dillion had us repaint that corridor outside her office about fifteen times. She kept saying the color wasn't right. In the end, she put the final coat on herself, all alone one night while everybody else was gone. I think it was her way of, you know, erasing things."

Aggie smiled faintly. "Yeah," she said. "I guess everybody has to do their own erasing."

He reached across the table and caught her pinkie with his, holding it briefly. "Give it a minute, Chief. You'll be surprised."

She gave his finger a grateful squeeze and sat back, sipping her milk. "This is what I can't figure out," she said thoughtfully. "Two senseless break-ins, both involving historical records, where nothing was taken except paper—something the thief could have gotten for free if he'd just waited until the offices were open."

"Yeah," Grady pointed out, "but then he'd have to show ID and sign in."

"And someone would be able to describe him— or her," she clarified, wanting to be fair, "in case there were questions later. Which is the same reason somebody would break into a hardware store and steal det cord—and a shovel, by the way—instead of just buying it."

"Well, one of the reasons," Grady countered dryly. "With the prices Keller charges, it'd be cheaper to face the B&E charge."

Aggie said, "Det cord is not something you'd generally expect to find while browsing your local Home Depot."

"Yeah," agreed Grady thoughtfully, "but every

contractor and farmer on the island knows Keller can get it for you."

"So we're looking for somebody local," Aggie suggested. "Maybe even somebody who's bought det cord from Keller before."

"There can't be that many people," Grady pointed out.

"Except…" Instead of finishing the sentence, Aggie just shook her head and said, "Mo thinks it's somebody from that protest group."

"What do you think?"

"I don't know," she admitted. "I'm not even sure the three crimes are related. And like you said, how would anybody who's not from around here even know to look for det cord in a hardware store?"

"You said that," he corrected. "But I'll take the credit."

Aggie opened the first folder and glanced over it. Daniel Micheal Jarvis, 28, B&E, possession with intent, multiple DUIs. The mug shot showed a scruffy looking, glazed-eyed kid with scraggly dark hair and a snake tattoo running from beneath his tee shirt up his neck. Aggie closed the file and opened another. Teton Lewis, age 32, Black and 220 pounds. She closed the file. River Keagan, age 26, B&E, multiple possession charges, probation violation, auto theft.

"Who names their kid River?" she murmured. "And what's he doing out, anyway?"

Grady shrugged. "Talk to the judge. It's like a damn revolving door around here."

Manny arrived with their lunch, and Aggie scooted

the files out of the way to make room. "Hey, Manny," she observed, "you're serving now. Good for you."

He grinned, setting her sandwich platter before her. "Only on off hours. And only for special customers."

He served Grady's food and placed a glass of ice water in front of each of them. Grady looked disapproving. "Next time," he said, "water first." Aggie kicked him under the table.

"Yes, sir, Captain Grady," Manny said, placing the extra plate of fries between them. "I'll remember."

He took the paper plate that held Flash's hamburger—no pickles, no ketchup, one piece of lettuce—and placed it on the floor beside him. "Can I get you anything else?"

Aggie held up her empty glass. "Maybe another one of these?"

Grady took the glass from her. "You're cut off," he said. As her brows knit, he added, "Far be it from me to criticize your cravings..."

"Very far," she agreed darkly.

"But babe, all that sugar. Enough, already." He turned to Manny. "Some more tartar sauce, when you get the chance."

"You got it, Captain. Be right back." Manny started to turn away and then looked back, his attention caught by the open folder beside Aggie's plate. "Is that guy wanted for something?" Then he gave a small shake of his head. "Man, I knew it."

Aggie, who was about to douse her fries in ketchup, put the bottle down and turned the folder toward him. "Do you recognize this man?"

"He was in here Saturday night," Manny said, "with some slick dude in a sports jacket. I noticed because, well, a sports jacket in this heat, yeah? And they seemed real—what's the word?—secret-like. Leaning close over the table, talking quiet. Then the sports jacket gave this guy some money. It looked like a drug deal to me, and I was about to tell the boss, because you know we don't allow that kind of stuff in Pete's Place. But by the time I did, they were gone." He frowned. "No tip."

"Did you see any drugs change hands?" Grady asked.

"Can you describe the man in the sports jacket?" Aggie said at the same time, widening her eyes at Grady. "My case," she reminded him.

"Yes, ma'am." Grady picked up the saltshaker and sprinkled its contents over his fries. But he did not pretend to lose interest in the conversation.

Manny replied diplomatically. "I didn't see any drugs. The man in the sports jacket, he had long hair, pulled back and tied. Maybe blond? Or light brown. Kind of thin on top. Not very big, white, no beard. Maybe 5'6", 140?" He thought for a moment. "He had soft hands. Not like a working man."

Flash, who had finished his beef patty—perfectly crunchy on the outside, almost raw in the middle— and was starting on the bun, looked up at this.

Grady asked, before Aggie could, "Have you ever seen him in here before?"

"No, sir, Captain," Manny replied. "But..." He

shrugged. "I don't know everyone yet."

Aggie said, "Any idea how much money was exchanged?"

Manny held his thumb and forefinger about half an inch apart. "Folded," he elucidated. "I couldn't see if it was twenties or fifties or what. But it looked like a lot."

Grady grunted thoughtfully and picked up his sandwich.

Aggie said, "You've got a good eye, Manny. Did you ever think about going into police work?"

Manny looked pleased. "You think so, Chief Aggie?"

"You have to be a US citizen," she pointed out.

"Yes, ma'am. Miss Lorraine, she helps me study on my breaks."

"Well, I can't hold the job open for you," Aggie said, "but when you get your bachelor's degree—and your citizenship—you let me know. Maybe we can work something out."

He grinned so broadly it looked as though his face might split. "Yes, ma'am!"

He turned back toward the kitchen, and Grady called after him, "Tartar sauce!"

Manny saluted him as he pushed open the kitchen door.

Grady said, "Person of interest?"

Aggie took a bite out of her sandwich. "I wouldn't mind talking to him." She chewed thoughtfully and swallowed. "Because if you *weren't* from around here and you *didn't* know where to find det cord, you might pay some shady ex-con like River Keagan to find it for you."

He lifted an eyebrow, acknowledging the possibility. "Or," he countered, "it could be just a routine drug buy."

"Which happened on my island." She squeezed ketchup on her plate and swirled a French fry in the puddle. "Have you got a last known location?"

"I'll text it to you. But do me a favor and send Mo. It's a pretty rough neighborhood."

Any other time Aggie would have bristled at the implication she couldn't take care of herself in a rough neighborhood, but today the mere thought of crossing the bridge in this heat made her woozy. "Yeah, okay. I have to run IDs on about twenty of those protestors, anyway, and check the security footage over the weekend to see if I can spot anybody suspicious coming in or out of the Grady building." Unfortunately, the only security cameras at the Grady warehouse building were in the parking lot and at the entrances. If anyone had entered the Records office over the weekend, there would be no video evidence of it.

"The thing is," Aggie said, chewing thoughtfully, "I don't think the perp meant to hurt Grace, just keep her out of the way. The ER doc said there was no sign of trauma—some bruises on her wrists and ankles from the tape, but that was all. Probably the guy didn't even realize there was no AC in the office when he locked her in. And that River character doesn't seem like the type to go easy on an old lady if she got between him and a job."

Grady turned the folder toward himself and flipped

a page. "You're right," he said, pointing midway down the page. "Two assaults. Subtle is not his style."

Aggie said, "Hmm." She finished half her sandwich and pushed the plate away. "Ryan," she said, "Bishop stayed to visit after you left."

"Yeah, I noticed." He nodded toward her plate. "Is that all you're going to eat?"

"Small, frequent meals," she reminded him. "So, what he wanted to talk about was…"

Grady's phone buzzed and he held up a finger for patience while he checked it. "Sorry, babe," he said, grabbing one more handful of fries as he put the phone away. "I've got to get back to it." He glanced around quickly as he stood, then kissed her lightly on the cheek. "Don't work too hard, okay?"

"Me? You're the one who hasn't finished a meal sitting down all day."

He winked at her and scooped up the remaining half of her sandwich. "See you tonight."

Aggie shared the rest of the French fries with Flash while she read through the suspects' jackets that Grady had left her. Her frown deepened the more she read. "I don't know, Flash," she said. "Two records office break-ins—related. Same MO, same time span, absolutely no motive. Hardware store—not related. But my gut tells me they're all the same thing, somehow." She looked at him. "What do you think?"

If there was one thing Flash did understand, it was that gut feeling. Cops talked about it all the time. Aggie said the gut feeling was hardly ever wrong because law officers were so highly trained, and so widely experienced with good things and bad, that their subconscious minds often picked up subtle clues their conscious brains didn't even register, and that they couldn't explain. It was called cop's instinct, and it was exactly the same thing Flash used every day. He had absolute faith in Aggie's gut instinct.

Aggie smiled and ruffled his ears. "Yeah, that's what I thought."

She stacked the folders, drained her water glass, and left a $5. 00 tip for Manny. Their break was over; time to get back to work.

CHAPTER FOURTEEN

Grady's car was in the driveway when Aggie arrived home that evening, much later than she had intended. She unbuckled her gun belt with stiff, aching fingers while Flash raced through the house to the kitchen, then she unlaced her shoes and kicked them off, leaving both in the front hall. She took a few deep breaths, straightened her shoulders, and marched into the kitchen with her arms outstretched.

"I," she declared, "am Supermom! I shut down a riot, saved a woman's life, sent four residents to the cooling shelter, and investigated three—count them—*three*—open cases. Didn't solve any of them, but still." She melted into her husband's arms. "Our daughter will be so proud."

He said, "Yeah, she will." He kissed her hair. "You're also exhausted, Supermom. Take a break."

She rested her cheek against his chest. "I am."

He said, "What about that lowlife, River Keagan?"

She roused herself to reply with an effort. "Not in residence when Mo stopped by. We'll take a fresh stab at it in the morning."

"Did you get anything on those beach bums?"

"No outstanding warrants," she replied. "That would have been too easy. A few misdemeanors and ordinance violations, about what you'd expect—public nuisance, disturbing the peace, noise..." She smothered a yawn. "Excessive noise. A couple of them were in the military, honorable discharges, but none of the prints I got from the historical society break-in matched. Same for the crowbar from the Keller job."

"But you've got DNA from the blood on the crowbar."

"Now all we need is a suspect."

She leaned against him for what felt like forever before adding, "So how did the rest of your day go?"

He shook his head, his chin rubbing against her hair. "I had to supervise an active shooter drill at the elementary school. I know they're necessary, but damn, I hate those things. One little girl was so scared she peed herself. It makes you wonder..." He let his voice trail off.

"What on earth we're thinking," Aggie supplied for him, "bringing a baby into this world? I was thinking the same thing this afternoon, talking to Mr. McMasters. He said it won't be long before fish are boiling in the ocean."

Flash, who had been enjoying a long drink from his

bowl, looked up in dismay. He had almost managed to put that image out of his mind.

Grady tightened his arms around her in a brief squeeze and kissed her hair. "Anyway," he said firmly, "that's not what I was wondering. I was wondering how we're going to fix everything that's wrong with the world in the six and a half months before she gets here."

Aggie laughed softly, kissed him, and stepped away. "I'm sorry I'm late. I stopped by the hospital to check on Grace Henderson."

"How is she?"

The smile that lingered from her husband's kiss faded away. "Still unconscious," she said. "The docs say it's up to her, now."

Grady said softly, "Damn. Anybody who'd do something like that to an old lady needs to be strung up by his balls."

"Yeah." This was spoken with a heavy breath. "Her daughter's driving down. Hopefully, there'll be good news by the time she gets here."

Aggie looked around the kitchen for the first time. The table was set with two place mats, two dishes, and silverware. There was even a candle. "Oh, Ryan," she said, dismayed. "It's my turn to make dinner. I was going to make fish tacos and watermelon salad."

He smiled. "Sounds great."

"Only I forgot to buy the fish. And the watermelon."

He chuckled softly and turned her toward the stairs. "I got this. Go shower and rest before dinner. I'll call you when it's ready."

She sighed. "Can I order a dozen more of you?"

"Don't get your hopes up." He gave her shoulder a playful push. "I'm taking a pack of hamburgers from the freezer. You want cheese on yours?"

"Cheese," she said. It took more effort than she had expected to move her feet toward the stairs. "I will love you forever."

He replied, "Same."

She barely heard him over the rattling of pots and pans as she made her way up the stairs.

Aggie showered and changed into shorts and a tee shirt, then decided to lie down just for a minute before going down to help with dinner. When she opened her eyes, Flash was pawing gently at her arm and the bedside clock said 8:04. For a moment she was so disoriented she didn't know if that was a. m. or p. m.

"Oh, no," she groaned, rolling out of bed. "The video call."

She splashed water on her face, swiped on a glaze of bronze lip gloss, and almost beat Flash down the stairs. She followed the sound of Grady's laugh and the tinny voices of the others to the kitchen, where he sat before the open laptop. Aggie ducked down to greet the family over his shoulder. "Hi, everybody!" she said a little breathlessly. "Sorry I'm late."

Ryan's parents, Lil and Salty Grady, had retired to Ecuador years before Aggie met Ryan, dividing most of their assets between their three children as an early inheritance. The house in which Aggie and Ryan now lived had once belonged to his parents and had been built by Ryan's grandfather—the same man for whom the Grady Memorial Bridge was named. The Gradys had spent the past winter in Dogleg Island and Aggie had fallen in love with them as thoroughly as she had with their son. Could she have survived the events of the winter without them? Probably. But she would not have survived whole. And neither would her husband.

Lil exclaimed from the video screen, "Oh, honey, we told Ryan not to wake you!"

And Salty added, "We know you need your baby sleep."

Lucy, Ryan and Pete's sister, remarked a little acerbically, "It's not as though the call hasn't been scheduled for over a week."

Lorraine rolled her eyes and muttered, "Oh, for heaven's sake." Lorraine was no bigger fan of Lucy's than Aggie was, but she had been in the family longer and felt less compunction about expressing her feelings.

"Now, Lucy," Lil said, mildly reprimanding. "You know perfectly well how it is the first few months. You slept twenty hours a day."

Lucy returned pertly, "I was carrying twins. It's hardly the same thing."

Pete appeared on the screen, sliding in beside Lorraine and settling Gabby on his knee. "Look who came to say hello," he said.

Gabby was dressed in a pink nightgown with her long dark hair caught up in two pink ribbons. She carried a black-and-white stuffed dog in her hands, and when she saw Aggie on the screen she thrust the dog forward, making it bounce like a playful pup.

Aggie laughed and called, "Flash!"

Flash came quickly and put his paws on the table next to the computer, grinning at Gabby. Gabby immediately began to sign something to Flash that was too fast for Aggie to understand. Flash, from all appearances, caught every word.

Lorraine pushed back a stray lock of Gabby's hair with tender amusement. "Gabby wanted to stay up to say goodnight to her *abuela* and *abuelo,* but it looks as though Flash is stealing the show. And tomorrow is a school day, so we need to mind our bedtime."

Aggie grinned. "She's the only six-year-old I know who's fluent in three languages—four, if you count canine. She should be teaching the class."

For the next few minutes everyone vied for Gabby's attention, signing their greetings to her to the best of their individual abilities. Flash went back to his place near the door, where he could listen to the conversation without being a distraction. When at last Lorraine called time on the visit, Salty and Lil blew their final kisses and Pete carried Gabby off to bed. Gabby waved goodbye with Flash the stuffed dog until she was off screen.

They spent a little more time talking about how adorable Gabby was and how much she had changed since Lil and Salty had seen her last. Then Salty said to Aggie, "You're not working too hard, are you, daughter? Have you managed to hire some help?"

Aggie replied, only mildly evasive, "Not yet. It's

hard to find the right person. And my office manager is leaving next week, so that's been a priority."

"Oh, please," said Lucy. "How hard can it be to replace that teenager?"

Lorraine, who had apparently had enough of Lucy's whining, interrupted, "We were just about to tell the folks all about the party this morning, Aggie."

"Which I wasn't invited to," Lucy put in.

There was a burst of chatter on the screen as everyone tried to talk at once—a fairly typical occurrence on these video calls—and Grady slipped his arm around Aggie's waist in a brief embrace. "I kept your dinner warm in the oven," he said. "Go eat."

Aggie was suddenly aware that her stomach felt hollow with hunger. "You're a saint," she whispered, and slipped away quickly while everyone was still talking.

Aggie ate quickly at the breakfast bar while the family catch-up went on behind her. Lucy's twins were spending the night with their father —to everyone's unspoken relief—as part of the custodial agreement Lucy had with her recently divorced husband. Lucy spent more than enough time lamenting the perils of being a single mother until Pete returned and abruptly cut her off with a change of subject.

Aggie finished off her hamburger—sharing the crusty parts with Flash—while Pete and Lorraine relayed the renovations on the Grady warehouse building and Ryan entertained them with funny stories about the lengths they'd all gone to in order to keep the party a surprise for Aggie. Aggie laughed along with everyone else, hearing the stories for the first time herself.

She spooned two scoops of ice cream into a glass and topped it with milk just as Ryan was saying, "And Aggie says Mr. Obadiah is selling the Shipwreck, can you believe that?"

Pete and Salty were lamenting the end of an era when Aggie, stirring her improvised milkshake with a straw, pulled up a chair close to Grady and joined them. "No offers yet," she assured them. "But no matter who buys it, it won't be the same."

Lil and Salty exchanged a look. They were sitting by their lagoon-style pool against the backdrop of a golden South American evening, lush tropical plants surrounding them, colorful tropical drinks on the table in front of them. The splashing of the pool's waterfall made a musical background noise, and somewhere in the distance a strange bird cawed. Lil gave a small secret smile and said, "Speaking of offers..."

Salty said importantly, "I suppose you're all wondering why we called this meeting."

Lorraine suggested, "Because you love us?"

And Pete said, leaning in, "What do you mean, offers? What's going on?"

Lil's smile broadened and she clasped her husband's hand. "We've had an offer on our place here!" she exclaimed. "We're moving!"

There was a clamor of everyone speaking at once: "What do you mean?" "Where will you go?" "When did this happen?" Flash put his paws on the table and edged his way between Aggie and Grady, eager to see what all the excitement was about.

Salty held up his hands for quiet, and when the last voice died down, he said, "Truth be told, we've been considering this for some time. The political situation here is not what it once was, and a lot of ex-pats are leaving. It doesn't feel as safe here as it once did."

Ryan and Pete nodded their approval, and Ryan said, "I can't say I disagree with you there, Dad."

Lil added, "And after being back in Florida this past winter, spending time with you all..." Again she glanced fondly at her husband. "We knew where we wanted to be. After all, we have four grandchildren now—well, almost four!—and why in the world would we want to miss another minute watching them grow up? So we're coming home!"

"Here?" cried Lorraine delightedly, clasping her hands together. "Back to Dogleg?"

Aggie exclaimed, "But your beautiful place!"

"Our beautiful place," replied Salty, waving an arm expansively, "just fetched four times what we paid for it. More than enough to persuade us to pack up our fine memories and say goodbye."

"And," put in Lil, beaming, "the buyer is kind enough to let us stay on until we can get everything packed up and shipped back to the States. But we'll be home for Christmas!"

There was another outburst of everyone talking at once, laughter and congratulations. Aggie hugged Flash, who grinned his excitement in return, and then she hugged Grady. "This is perfect!" she said. "Oh, I'm so glad!"

Lorraine hugged Pete and declared, "We couldn't be happier! You know we've wanted you back here for years!"

And Pete, grinning, said, "I swear to God, Dad, you always did have the luck of the Irish when it came to real estate. Good for you!"

It was Lucy who pointed out practically, "Where are you going to live?"

"Well," replied Salty, "we still have that pretty piece of property across the lagoon from Pete, and I've been talking to George Cooper about building us a house there. He says he can have it ready by early next summer."

"In the meantime," put in Lil, "we were hoping Ryan and Aggie wouldn't mind letting us use their little guest house again."

"Yes!" replied Aggie immediately. "Of course! Yes!"

"Well, I like that," put in Lucy, disgruntled. "You build your house next to Pete, you move into Ryan's guest house... when do I get to see you? And my boys?"

"Whenever you want, honey," Lil replied soothingly. "We'll only be fifteen minutes away."

"Which is not the same as a continent," Salty pointed out, "like we are now."

"But why do you have to move to the island?" Lucy insisted. "There's a lot more to do here in Ocean City, and the taxes are lower, too. Not to mention you'd be closer to medical care and golf courses and the senior center..."

Once again Lorraine made no attempt to disguise an eyeroll, and Aggie coughed into her hand to hide a chuckle.

Salty said, "Thank you, my lovely, for making us feel even older than we are, but our minds are made up. Dogleg Island is home, and that's where we're going."

They spent a few more minutes chatting about specifics before agreeing that it would take many more such calls to work out all the details of the move. Aggie and Ryan were, by design, the last to sign off.

Aggie said, "You can't know what a relief it is, just knowing you'll be here when the baby is born."

Lil beamed happily, patting her husband's hand. "We were there to welcome the twins into the world, and we were there to welcome Gabby into the family. Of course we'll be there for this little one."

"You couldn't keep us away," Salty assured her.

Ryan grinned at Aggie. "Built-in babysitters, right in our own backyard."

"You can for certain count on that," replied Salty with a companionable wink at his wife.

Aggie said, "Salty, while I've got you... I wonder if you remember anything about the Mercury oil spill back in 1980."

Salty pursed his lips with a regretful shake of his head. "I heard plenty about it, I can tell you, but thank the Lord I wasn't here when it happened. My sweet girl and I were stationed in Hawaii at the time."

"With a three-year-old and another on the way," Lil

reminded him. "Lucy was born in the base hospital."

Aggie said, "I heard there was some kind of problem when the oil company started building Mercury Park. Something about the military shutting it down?"

His brow furrowed thoughtfully. "Well, now, I do seem to recall some kind of scandal, but the details escape me. Like I say, we weren't based on the mainland then. If I had to guess, though, it might have had something to do with government-owned land. The military did have an interest in the island during World War II, I know. Used it for maneuvers and weapons testing right up through the sixties." He gave another shake of his head. "Sorry I can't be of more help, darlin'. But if it's important, I'll bet you Jess Krieger would know. He keeps everything that's ever been published about Dogleg, back from before he even took over the paper."

Aggie smiled. "That's a great idea, Salty. Thanks."

A wave of fatigue swept over her unexpectedly, and she had to blink her eyes several times to maintain her focus. Ryan, sensing this, cupped a hand around her knee.

"Okay, folks, I think we've all had enough excitement for one night. More than enough for some, if you get my drift." He slanted his eyes meaningfully toward Aggie, who elbowed him in the ribs. A continent away, his parents laughed good-naturedly.

"Good night, my daughter," Salty said.

Aggie loved it when he called her that.

"You take care, honey," Lil added, blowing a kiss.

"And remember, you absolutely, positively can't get too much sleep at this stage. It's nature's way of making up for what you'll be missing when the baby comes."

Aggie said, "I love you both. And I'm so happy you're coming home."

Two hours later, Grady climbed into bed in tee shirt and boxers and turned on his bedside lamp, saying, "I think you're my parents' new favorite child."

"It's just because I'm new."

Aggie slipped out of the shorts and tee shirt and checked in the bathroom mirror for any sign of a baby bump. Nothing yet. She pulled on a nightshirt and returned to the bedroom, switching off the overhead light as she did. The ceiling fan whirred gently overhead, blocking the sound of the ocean that was her usual lullaby. Flash was stretched out near the air-conditioning vent beside their bed, his favorite spot during the summer. She bent to rub his ears as she passed.

"I don't know why I'm so tired," she said, clambering into bed beside her husband. "I can hardly keep my eyes open."

Grady reached for the copy of *What to Expect When You're Expecting* that he kept on his nightstand. "On page 21 it says..."

Aggie placed her palm over the open page. "I know what it says on page 21."

She scrunched close to him and punched down her pillow under her cheek. "You know, Ry, I don't mind saying I've been a little scared about this whole baby thing. You know, we wanted this so long, and all the doctors said don't get our hopes up, and now I can't help wondering... are we pushing our luck?"

He took her hand and kissed her fingers, holding her eyes. "We're not pushing our luck," he told her firmly. "We've been through hell, and we've proven that nothing this little guy—I mean gal—can throw at us will shake us, so we're ready."

She looked at him anxiously. "It's just that... maybe we shouldn't have been so quick to tell people. Maybe we should've waited until the third trimester was over, like Lucy said. Maybe we shouldn't have, you know... tempted fate."

Grady's hand tightened on her fingers, and he said gently, "We talked about this. Keeping it a secret would be like pretending she didn't exist. And I, for one, want to enjoy every minute I have with her, and I want other people to enjoy her too. Because the more people who love her..."

"The happier she'll be to come into the world," Aggie finished softly. She kissed her husband's lips. "I love you, Ryan Grady."

He smiled and kissed her back. "For what it's worth, I've been a little scared too."

Aggie took a breath. "But now that your mom is coming," she said, "I feel better. Calmer. Like everything is going to be all right."

He kissed her again. "Me, too."

He opened the book again and turned the page. "What was all that about Mercury Park?"

"Oh, just something that protestor dude said." Her voice was sleepy. "And then Mr. McMasters confirmed it."

"Send me what you've got on the leader," Ryan said. "I'll do a deep dive for you tomorrow."

"That would save me some time. Thanks."

He turned another page. Aggie blinked hard to keep her eyes open.

"Ryan," she said, "I need to tell you something, but I'm too tired to discuss it tonight. So just listen."

He put the book aside and looked at her cautiously. "Okay."

"Bishop is retiring," she said.

He sat up straight, staring at her. "And he told you and not me?"

"He told me because he didn't want to blindside you."

He scowled. "About what?"

"He wants you to run for sheriff," she said. "The filing deadline is Friday."

He held her gaze with absolutely no expression for a long time, and then he sank back against the pillow.

"It's a lot more money," Aggie said. "I mean, a *lot* more. And Bishop thinks you can win. I do too."

He said, "I'm not a politician."

"I know."

"And it's the kind of job that only lasts four years. What if I don't get reelected?"

"Friday," she murmured, her eyes closed.

He was silent for a while, frowning thoughtfully. Then he said, "It makes sense, I guess. I mean, I know Bishop's always had me in mind for this. We all knew he wouldn't stay in office forever, and he never promised us four more years. It's just... man." He ran his fingers through his sun-bleached hair with an exhaled breath. "It still just feels like it came out of nowhere, you know?"

Again he let the silence fall. When he resumed, his tone was ruminating. "But you're right. The money would make all the difference, with the baby coming." He smiled to himself. "And I guess it would be a lot more fun on career day to say 'my daddy's the sheriff' than 'my daddy rides around in a patrol car giving out tickets.' But, babe, you know I've never been that good behind a desk, and..."

He turned his head on the pillow to look at her, but Aggie was sound asleep.

Flash, basking in the cool air that flowed from the floor vent, was thinking over the events of the day. He was happy Lil and Salty were coming home; Salty told great stories and Lil smelled better than anyone he knew except Aggie. Of course, he had always known they would be back. Some things were just wrong, and seeing Lil and Salty trapped inside a tiny computer screen was one of them.

He thought briefly about crabs in cages and fish in the ocean, and about the angry people at the beach who wanted to save the ocean... although from what, he wasn't sure they had ever explained. Mostly he thought about locks. The broken locks on the records office and Mr. Keller's store, the lock Mo had broken to save Mrs. Henderson. He thought about how things like broken locks so often came together in a group, and like pieces of a broken picture, they sometimes told a story if you looked at them long enough. Or sometimes they didn't.

He hoped that tomorrow all the locks would be open.

CHAPTER FIFTEEN

Grady had an early call, so Aggie made oatmeal and bananas for breakfast. That was not Flash's favorite, but he didn't want to hurt her feelings, so he ate most of it along with a few bites of kibble to keep him going until lunch. They had a busy morning, and he was anxious to get going.

The air smelled like salt, and a warm wind slicked back his fur as Flash stepped outside. The incoming tide thundered against the shore two blocks away. Aggie combed her hair away from her face and looked up at the sky, eyes narrowed. "Maybe I should have turned on The Weather Channel," she said, opening the car door for Flash. "We might get some rain today."

But even though the sun was barely bright enough to show the color of the sky, Flash could have told her there was no rain in the forecast. Rain was one of those things he could smell. He used to wonder why Aggie couldn't smell it too, but then he realized she didn't have to. She had him.

The trip across the bridge to the hospital took

eighteen minutes, and the buffeting of the wind as they crossed the water made Aggie's knuckles go white on the steering wheel. After all this time, she still wasn't comfortable crossing the bridge, and she didn't think she ever would be. She was glad she had stuffed her pockets with Mo's ginger candies, and she popped one in her mouth as soon as she parked in front of the hospital, taking a moment to settle her stomach and finger-comb her hair before getting out of the car.

She left the air-conditioning running for Flash and told him, "This shouldn't take long." In fact, Aggie wasn't even sure she would be able to get in to see Grace Henderson this early in the day, or if she was capable of having visitors at all. But with any luck at all, Aggie would at least be able to talk to the woman's daughter.

The hospital corridor was early-morning quiet as Aggie made her way to room 236. She knocked lightly on the door before pushing it open, and was gratified to see Grace Henderson propped up in her hospital bed in a semi-sitting position with a breakfast tray before her. She was deathly pale, with IVs in both arms and an oxygen cannula in her nose, but she was awake. A younger woman sat on the bed next to her, holding a cup with a straw to Grace's lips. "Come on, Mama," she was saying when Aggie entered. "Just a little more juice."

Grace turned her head away weakly, and Aggie said, "Excuse me. I'm Aggie Malone, Chief of Police on Dogleg Island. Are you Mrs. Henderson's daughter?"

The woman put the glass down and turned, looking surprised. "Oh, Chief. Yes. I'm Ellie Whitmire. Did we speak on the phone? I'm sorry. It's been a long night."

Ellie Whitmire was in her forties, although a sleepless night spent driving down from Ohio had etched lines into her face that made her look older. She wore a wrinkled tee shirt, jeans and sandals, and her brunette hair was escaping its ponytail in frizzy tendrils.

Aggie smiled as she came farther into the room. "That's okay," she said. "I'm sorry to bother you this early in the morning, but I was hoping to have a word with your mother. I'm glad to see she's awake."

Ellie returned the smile uncertainly. "This might not be the best time. She's still a little... disoriented."

Aggie said, "I understand. I'll be brief."

Ellie touched her mother's cheek lightly and said, "Mama, look who's here to see you. It's the police chief. She wants to talk to you for a minute, okay?"

Grace Henderson's eyes fluttered open, her gaze wandering the room for a moment before settling on Aggie. "Oh, hello, dear," she said weakly. "Have you met my daughter, Ellie?"

"Hi, Mrs. Henderson." Aggie stood at the foot of the bed. "I'm so glad to see you sitting up. How are you feeling?"

"Oh, I'm fine." She fluttered a finger, but could not lift her hand from the bed. "A little tired."

"I won't stay long," Aggie promised. "I wonder if you could tell me what happened Sunday."

She frowned faintly. "Sunday?"

"At the historical society," Aggie prompted. "You went there and got locked in."

She seemed troubled. "Oh, I don't think so. We're not open on Sunday. You'll have to come back Tuesday. It's on the sign."

Aggie glanced at the daughter, who returned her look helplessly.

Aggie said, "Did someone come in while you were there, Mrs. Henderson? Or maybe someone was already there when you arrived?"

She merely looked puzzled.

Aggie tried again, "Mrs. Henderson, it's really important that you try to remember what happened. Can you tell me anything at all about the person who hurt you?"

She replied, "Oh, I'm fine, dear. Have you met my daughter, Ellie? She came all the way down here to see me."

Ellie patted her mother's hand. "Why don't you try to rest a little, Mama? I'm going to go talk to the chief for a minute. I'll be right outside the door."

Aggie told Grace Henderson, "Get better, Mrs. Henderson. I'll check on you later."

In the corridor, Ellie Whitmire hugged her arms, her face creased with worry. "The doctors aren't sure how extensive the damage is. She has an MRI scheduled for this afternoon."

"I'm so sorry," Aggie said, and meant it.

"She hasn't been able to remember anything about the weekend, and she gets confused about some things that happened before that." Ellie looked at Aggie, her expression pleading. "Do you have any idea who did this? How did this happen? Why?"

Aggie said, "Our best working theory is that your mother intercepted someone who had broken into the historical society offices. We don't know what they were looking for. They tied your mother up and taped her mouth just to get her out of the way. It's possible," she added, because she thought it would make the daughter feel better, "they didn't realize there was no air-conditioning. They might not have intended to leave her in a life-threatening situation."

The other woman's lips compressed bitterly. "Well, it doesn't matter what they *intended*, now does it? What kind of place is this, anyway? What kind of people live here?"

"Mostly good ones," Aggie assured her. "And I promise we're going to do everything in our power to find whoever did this to your mother and bring them to justice. In the meantime..." She took a card from her pocket and handed it to the other woman. "If she happens to remember anything, or if you can think of anything that might help, my cell phone is on this card. Call any time."

Flash didn't particularly like waiting in the air-conditioning, even though he knew it was part of the job, but he didn't complain because Aggie always updated him. This time, she had very little to report.

"So," she said, sinking into her seat behind the wheel, "no eyewitness." She dug another candy out of her pocket and popped it into her mouth. "No one we've talked to so far can think of any reason anyone would want to hurt Grace Henderson, so it looks like whoever broke in was just trying to keep her out of the way while he looked for what he wanted. I say we check with Nora Billings and see if she's been able to find out what he was after."

Flash was onboard with any plan that kept the case moving forward, and he sat up straight, taking his position at the passenger window, as Aggie started the engine. She was just exiting the parking lot when her phone rang. She put it on speaker.

Grady said, "Hey, Chief. Are you still beachside?"

"Just headed back that way from the hospital. What's up?"

His voice was grim. "We pulled a body out of the harbor on Tenth Street this morning. I think you're going to want to see this."

Aggie said, "On my way."

CHAPTER SIXTEEN

Flash dug in his claws as Aggie turned left instead of right and swung out into traffic. They were at the Ocean City harbor in less than four minutes. Aggie drove past the sprawling marina, where all the private boats were docked, and followed the flashing lights past a row of low weathered buildings across from the dock where the commercial fishing boats tied up. Most of the boats left at dawn, so the slots were sparsely occupied. Aggie saw several deputies talking to someone who was apparently the captain of one of the boats. He kept looking impatiently over his shoulder, anxious to be on his way.

There were five sheriff's cruisers, an ambulance, and the coroner's van crowding the narrow roadway, all with lights strobing and radios crackling. Flash powered down the window with his paw and leapt out as soon as their SUV stopped, eagerly taking in the scents of fish and motor oil and warm mist off the water; bait buckets and salty rope and the tinny scent of blood—fish blood, and human blood, and something even worse: that dark, cold-rot smell that always made his fur stand on end, that always made him want to go somewhere and hide.

Grady came toward them as Aggie got out of the car. He was part of the sheriff's office dive team, and he still wore his wet suit, unzipped to the waist over his gray department-issue tee shirt. Flash could smell that wet, dark smell on him, and Aggie, seeing her husband's face, knew why he had been pulled out of bed on an early call this morning.

The wind was not as strong here as it had been beachside, but it tossed Aggie's hair around and briefly plastered her uniform shirt to her body when she stepped out of the car. She took her cap from the console and placed it firmly on her head, walking toward Grady. He met her halfway.

Grady nodded toward the fisherman who was being interviewed by the deputies. "Jed Riley was getting ready to take his shrimp boat out this morning when he noticed something knocking against his hull. He turned on his flashlight and saw what appeared to be a body beneath the surface." He touched her shoulder, indicating they should walk down the dock toward the emergency vehicles. "By the time we got here the current had carried the body under the boat. It was caught up in a piece of broken net; otherwise we might not have found it for days. Took a while for us to get him up."

He gestured toward the coroner's van, and they wove their way between patrol cars to reach a gurney with the figure of a man stretched out atop a black body bag. Sea water had dampened the concrete beneath the stretcher and for several feet around it. Two technicians were about to zip up the body bag, but Grady held up a hand to stop them. Aggie started forward. Flash held back. He could smell the cold decay from here.

Aggie looked down at the corpse. The face was pale, the skin shrunken like wax over the bones and mottled with the dark splotches of death, but the features were recognizable. "River Keagan," she said. She pointed to a reddish-brown indentation on the side of his head, about four inches in diameter, where pieces of bone were visible. "Cause of death?"

Grady stood beside her, his expression tight. "You know Sam. He won't commit to anything." He referred to the county coroner who, as he repeatedly told law enforcement every time he was called out to certify death, was not a medical examiner. "But the wound was pre-mortem, and it's the working theory that the blow to head sent him into the water. Best guess is it happened sometime last night."

Aggie looked around, noticing evidence tags marking off a stain on the pier a dozen yards away, along with several other tags at various locations along the pier. "Murder weapon?"

He shook his head. "Not yet. We searched the water but it's pretty murky down there. We'll give it a few more tries."

Aggie said, "Could have been a drug deal gone bad. Or a disagreement over some other felony."

"Most likely was," Grady agreed. "But I thought you'd want to know."

Aggie's gaze traveled thoughtfully back over the lifeless body. Faded blue tee shirt advertising a beer brand, ripped jeans, frayed sneakers, all soaking wet and stained with mud and seaweed. Sharp, foxlike face, a crew cut so short it was almost shaved. And a raw scrape on the back of his left hand.

Aggie looked around for the coroner, who was packing up his equipment near the van. She waved him over, and he came with a reluctant expression on his face. "Chief," he said, "like I told the deputies, I can't pinpoint time of death…"

"This wound on his hand," Aggie interrupted. "Did he get it before he died?"

Sam glanced at the place she indicated. "Yes, I saw that, photographed it. It looks to me like it had started to heal there around the edges, some swelling, too, so I'd say it's a day or two old. But I can't make an official determination…"

"Thanks, Sam," Aggie said. She popped another candy into her mouth.

Grady looked at her carefully. "You feeling okay?"

"Oh, please. I've got a stronger stomach ten weeks pregnant than you do on an average Tuesday."

"No argument there," he said. The corners of his lips were lined and pale. "Let's get out of here."

The technicians zipped up the body bag, and Aggie

walked with Grady toward the evidence markers. As soon as the body was rolled toward the van, Flash caught up with Aggie.

"Mr. Obadiah said the guy who came in before dawn yesterday morning to buy fishing line had a cut on his left hand," Aggie said. "He matched Keagan's description, too, down to the tee shirt."

"You're thinking he's the one who broke into Keller's?"

"Maybe," Aggie said thoughtfully. "And maybe somebody paid him to do it."

"The guy Manny saw him with at Pete's," Grady supplied.

"That'd be my guess."

"He had two hundred in twenties on him," Grady said, "folded together like they'd come that way."

"So maybe he came here to deliver the goods and get the rest of his money. Instead, he got hit on the head with a blunt object."

"Or it could have been a drug deal gone bad."

"Most likely," agreed Aggie.

Grady pointed to the first evidence marker and the six-inch diameter stain beside it. "Initial point of impact," he said. He gestured to several other, smaller blood droplets around it. "Residual spatter, possibly from the backswing of the weapon." He gestured to the raised concrete wall of the dock, where another marker stood. "This is where he went over, either from the force of the blow or being pushed. That's where we're searching for the weapon."

Flash checked out each marker and moved on,

discovering nothing worth lingering over. Aggie watched as Flash sniffed the tires of a battered blue Nissan pickup truck. The dock was too narrow to fully park on the concrete, so it was pulled sloppily half onto the weedy ground abutting the pier. "Is that his vehicle?"

"Near as we can tell. We're tracking down the registration now. There's another set of fresh tracks in the ground next to it." He pointed to another evidence marker. "Bigger vehicle, full-size truck or SUV. We figure it belonged to the perp."

Flash carefully avoided the evidence markers and made his way deeper into the weeds. Aggie watched him thoughtfully. "You've got to admit," she said, "it's pretty interesting that the one person I wanted to interview turns up dead less than twenty-four hours after Mo goes looking for him."

"More than interesting," Grady said. "But I'm not buying that a misdemeanor break-in was worth Keagan's life. My guess is he was into something bigger, and Mo's visit yesterday made somebody a little too nervous."

"Do you suppose that 'something bigger' might be possession of stolen explosives?"

"Very possibly."

A gust of wind threatened to snatch Aggie's cap from her head, and she caught it quickly. "What's up with this wind?"

"Outer bands of a tropical storm in the Gulf," Grady replied. He was something of a weather junkie, a side-effect of being, as he described it, born to sail. "Winds gusting up to 30 today and tomorrow. No rain 'til Thursday, though, if then."

"Too bad. I never thought I'd see the day when I'd be hoping for a little tropical storm."

"Yeah, me too." Grady followed Aggie's gaze as she watched Flash explore the ground. "What's he up to?"

"I'm not sure."

"He'd better be careful. Plenty of sandspurs out there."

"Flash is always careful."

He smiled at her. "What did you have for breakfast?"

"Oatmeal and bananas. What about you?"

"Donuts."

She made a scoffing sound. "And you dare talk to me about sugar. I'm shopping for a new dietary manager."

"I'm hurt."

In a moment Aggie said, "Any leads on who might have been interested in acquiring det cord yesterday?"

"We're running it down, but so far, nothing. You?"

She shook her head, watching Flash. "Mo's keeping her ear to the ground, checking out the less-reputable prospects on the back side of the island, but this time of the year we know most everybody on the island and none of them fit the particulars." Then she added absently, "Hold on a minute." She followed Flash into the weeds.

Flash had found what he was looking for about ten yards away and stood patiently waiting for Aggie. Aggie took a glove from her back pocket and picked up the crumpled, blood-stained paper from the ground. She didn't have to unfold it to recognize what it was.

Grady stood beside her. "It's one of those flyers from the protestors," he said.

"Not just one." Even as she spoke, the wind blew several of the flyers, which were scattered across the ground in various directions, even farther away. Flash started to chase them, but she said, "It's okay, Flash. Leave it."

He came back to her side, disappointed. Chasing was one of his best things.

Grady raised his arm and called back to one of the officers, "Jefferson! Camera and evidence bags!"

Aggie examined the crumpled paper in her hand. "Looks like he used it to wipe the murder weapon—or maybe even his hands. When he opened the car door, the wind must have blown the rest of the fliers out."

"The wind started kicking up some time after midnight," Grady said. "But, Aggie, these things are all over town."

"Yeah, but not everybody is carrying a whole bunch of them around in his car." When the officer arrived with the evidence bags, she placed the blood-stained flyer inside one and returned it to him for sealing. "I think I'll have another talk with everybody's favorite troublemakers."

CHAPTER
SEVENTEEN

Dogleg Island was so named because of its shape. The narrow, angular "leg" of the island that connected to the mainland via the Grady Memorial Bridge was mostly sandy beach, while the wider "haunch" of the island was pine forest and wetlands. This part of the island, formerly a turpentine plantation, was mostly undeveloped parkland or wilderness area now with the majority devoted to a wildlife preserve at the far eastern end of the island. There were a few businesses along the packed sand road that led to the preserve—a stable that rented horses for beach riding, a small charter fishing service—and a few isolated homes or trailer homes set back in the woods off the main road.

Mercury Park was a pleasant little gem located on the haunch end of the island between the riding stables and the wildlife preserve. Though it was mostly day use, it accommodated a privately maintained campground that offered primitive tent camping only. There were several miles of hiking and bike trails, a wide bridle path that meandered through the dunes, and picnic tables scattered throughout. Beach access was via several narrow, sandspur-riddled paths. Admission was free to the public; campsites charged a nominal fee.

The campground hosts rotated seasonally and were responsible only for keeping the restrooms clean and collecting fees. There was no gate, just a sign that said: *Campers, check in at office.* Aggie did not expect anyone to be in the office at 7:45 in the morning when she and Flash arrived, so she drove right past the little concrete block building. Straight ahead was the day use park, a pretty spot of green shaded by live oaks and wind-twisted pines, dotted with picnic tables and featuring a children's playground. In the center was a large granite sphere with wings on each side, the emblem of the Mercury Oil company. The plaque on its base read, "Mercury Memorial Park, dedicated for the enjoyment of the people of Dogleg Island in the year of Our Lord 1986." In the distance she could see the geodesic dome of the newly constructed Mercury Environmental Center. Just past the park the road split four ways, with signs pointing to camping, beach, nature trails, and environmental center. Aggie turned toward tent camping.

The campground was a narrow half acre set on a slight rise covered with spotty grass, wild lantana, and sand. The beach was a quarter mile away, but there was a sand path leading to it. A long green building marked "showers" stood on the opposite side of the road from the campsites. A young woman, coming from the showers with a towel and a scrub bag in her hand, gave Aggie a hard look as she pulled up.

There were at least a dozen tents scattered throughout the campground, and the smell of campfire smoke greeted Aggie and Flash as they got out of the car. Lawn chairs were drawn up around a firepit, and a plastic tablecloth flapped in the wind on one of the picnic tables. Only four heavy stones at the corners kept it from flying away. There were quite a few people up and about, trying to make coffee on a park grill or carrying paper bowls of cereal to the picnic table to eat. Most of them Aggie recognized from the beach demonstration yesterday, and if she hadn't, the suspicious looks on their faces as she passed would have reminded her.

Cade Rodan, the apparent leader of the group, came down the path from the beach wearing damp board shorts and carrying a beach towel. His close-cropped hair still sparked with dampness and, as he grew closer, Aggie couldn't help noticing a flesh-colored bandage on the back of his hand.

"Mr. Rodan," she greeted him. "I see you're enjoying the beautiful beaches of Dogleg Island bright and early this morning."

"I figure we all better enjoy them while we can," he replied easily. "They'll be gone soon enough."

This was the part of an investigation Flash liked least: the questioning of suspects. For one thing, suspects hardly ever told the truth, so questioning them never did much good. Not like, for example, a crowbar with blood on it or a bunch of papers scattered by the wind that had the very same blood on them. And for another thing, suspects very often said things that made no sense, like Cade saying the beaches would soon be gone. Where did he think they were going? Flash had the unhappy feeling this was all going to lead to nothing except more to wonder about when he was pondering the unanswerable in his head.

Aggie said, "What happened to your hand?"

He glanced at the bandage on his hand, clearly surprised she had noticed. "I banged it against a jetty yesterday."

"There aren't any jetties on this part of the beach," Aggie pointed out.

"I didn't say I was swimming here," he replied, frowning a little. "Did you come all the way out here to ask about my health?"

"That," she admitted, "and to ask where you were last night between 10:00 p. m. and 5:00 a. m."

The frown deepened. "Here, sleeping, like everybody else. We had a meeting to plan today's rally, then everybody went to bed around 10:30. What's this about?"

"Was everybody at that meeting?"

He shrugged. "I didn't count heads."

She said, "Did anybody leave the camp during the night?"

"How the hell should I know? Look, Chief, we cooperated when your officer came by yesterday collecting everybody's IDs, even though she had absolutely no right to do so. But if you're going to start harassing us for every little thing that goes wrong on this island, I have legal recourse."

"Those flyers you've been passing out all over town," Aggie said. "Who's in charge of them?"

He looked both annoyed and confused. "What do you mean, in charge?"

"I mean, who keeps stacks of them to pass out?"

"We all do," he replied impatiently. "That's the point—to get the information about the rally into as many hands as possible. Some of the citizens take stacks, too, to put up in shop windows and pass out at meetings and all."

Aggie took out her phone and brought up River Keagan's mug shot. "Do you know this man?"

He glanced at it in annoyance. "No. And he doesn't look like somebody I'd want to know, either."

She put her phone away, glancing around. Hostile faces stared back at her from far and near. "I'm going to want to talk to all of your people before you head out this morning."

He replied impatiently, "They're not 'my people. ' We're here because we all believe in the same thing and want to do something to break the hold corporate greed has on our way of life."

It sounded like something he was quoting from a protest manual, but at least it was a semblance of an explanation for what, exactly, they were protesting. Aggie said, "What does that have to do with Dogleg Island?"

"Come to the rally and find out," he answered.

"Oh, I'll be there," she promised. "Along with a half-dozen sheriff's deputies." Or at least she hoped so.

"As long as they don't interfere with our right to free speech," he replied breezily, "they're more than welcome. And oh, by the way, it's not just 'my' people, as you say, who are interested in the future of Dogleg Island. We're expecting at least a hundred residents to join us this afternoon."

"What are you doing?" Aggie returned irritably. "Serving refreshments?"

He just chuckled and turned to go.

"We're looking for stolen explosives," Aggie said.

He turned around, and it was impossible to miss the flicker of alarm that crossed his eyes. Alarm, yes, but not surprise. "What?"

"That's a felony," Aggie replied. "And so is concealing knowledge of such stolen explosives."

He looked uneasy. "What has that got to do with us?"

"I'm sure I couldn't say," Aggie said. "But if you notice a larger-than-ordinary police presence on the island, that's why. And, of course, if you should come across any information that would be helpful in our search, you'll be obligated to let us know. To do otherwise would be the commission of a class-three felony." She held his gaze for a moment, letting that sink in. "Have a good day. And," she added before she started off toward the nearest campsite, "make sure all these fires are out before you leave. We're under a no-burn order."

"Hey, Chief."

Aggie looked back.

The young man appeared to be struggling to hold on to his previous cockiness, and his eyes looked worried. "Listen, I just want to be clear about something. None of this is my idea. I mean, I didn't organize this demonstration. I never even heard of Dogleg Island until we were told to come here."

Aggie said, "Told by who?"

"Look," he said, frustrated, "these things don't just happen, you know. They have to be organized, paid for, and that's not something anybody here is involved in. So when you talk about somebody being responsible, it's not me."

"Then who?" Aggie persisted.

He shifted his gaze away uncomfortably, and then back. "There's a lot of them online, you know? They recruit people to..." he fumbled for the words.

"Agitate the populace?" suggested Aggie.

"Get their message out," he corrected, now sounding more annoyed than defensive. "You can go to the website, sign up, and they pay your travel expenses, a stipend for meals and stuff, and guarantee bail if you get picked up."

Aggie glanced around. "Whoever's backing you must be doing it on a budget."

He gave a brief half-grin. "Yeah, but it's at the beach."

"So who's your sponsor?"

The grin faded again into discomfiture, as though he was not entirely sure he should be revealing the name of his benefactor. "Some environmental organization called the Dover Group."

Aggie made a note. "Name?"

He shook his head. "Nobody in particular, at least that I've been in contact with. They supply the literature and the game plan, we send daily updates. You can check out their website. It's legit."

One of the things Aggie always said was that when a subject was in the mood to talk, the best thing to do was let him talk. The other thing she said was that there was nothing a nervous person hated more than silence. Flash had never known her to be wrong about this—or anything, really—and, sure enough, as she just stood there, letting the silence wear on, Cade eventually rushed to fill it.

"Okay," he said, "there's this one guy, Aaron Fisher, you could talk to him. He's not really with us, just follows us around and interviews us for this podcast he does. He seems to have contacts with the Dover Group. He can probably answer your questions."

Aggie made a note. "Where can I find him?"

"At the end of the row. Site 21, I think. He's got a fifth wheel camper. They let him bring it in because of the podcast."

Aggie wrote that down, and again she waited. Cade shifted his weight back and forth on the balls of his feet, and his gaze roamed around in counter-rhythm.

"Look," he said, "maybe I heard somebody coming in this morning before light. I didn't get up to look. It's an open park, no gate. The sign says it closes at dusk, but nobody pays attention to it. Maybe a new camper,

I don't know. That's all I know. Now, if you don't mind, it's getting late, and I've got a lot to do."

He moved past them, and Aggie let him go. Flash was glad. As important as he knew it was to listen, he had much rather be moving.

"Interesting," Aggie remarked as they walked away, "how cooperative he got when I mentioned a felony charge. Maybe there's something in his background we missed."

Cade went to a campsite about twenty feet down the path and ducked inside a tent. There was a silver pickup truck parked near the tent in a narrow parking spot. The tailgate was down, but the bed of the truck was covered with a blue tarp. While Aggie stopped a woman who was headed toward a nearer tent, Flash went to explore.

The thing about patterns was that the more parts to the pattern there were, the clearer the pattern became. Pretty soon, when all the parts came together, the pattern would be complete. First there was the crowbar, then the paper, and now this. Patterns. He loved them.

Aggie found Flash two brief interviews later with his paws on the open tailgate of the truck, waiting for her. Aggie looked at the closed tent flap a half-dozen yards away, nestled in a pine cove, and then at the tarp covering the pickup's bed. She ran a hand over Flash's head, murmuring, "Something I need to see, bud?"

She looked back toward the tent again, seeming to debate something in her mind. Then she shook her head. "Unlawful search and seizure, Flash. Unless you've found drugs in there, we have to let it go... for now."

Reluctantly, Flash dropped his front paws to the ground. There were no drugs. Finding the pattern was much more important than finding drugs, in his opinion, but then there was that word again: *law*. The thing only Aggie understood.

He walked with Aggie a few feet away to the next campsite, where a bearded man was getting into his car. Aggie showed the man the picture on her phone and asked if he had heard anyone come into the campsite early this morning. He said no. Flash kept an eye on the truck with the blue tarp. So, he noticed, did Aggie as they went to the next person and asked the same questions. Flash noticed Cade Rodan carrying a cooler from his tent to his truck. So did Aggie. They walked back to the truck and reached it just as Cade was untying the tarp. This time Flash took no chances. He leapt up into the bed of the truck just as Cade was swinging his cooler inside, and he stood there, waiting for Aggie.

"Hey!" Cade looked around for Aggie, saw her, and gestured with his shoulder to Flash. "Your dog!"

Aggie looked over the contents of the truck bed. There was a surfboard, a couple of empty clear plastic containers that had probably contained camping supplies, a toolbox, and a shovel. The shovel still had the yellow price tag on it from Keller's Hardware, and a smear of something reddish brown on the handle near the blade.

Aggie said, "Is this your truck?"

Flash jumped down and Cade put the cooler inside. "Yeah, it's mine. Are you about done here?"

Aggie gestured to the shovel. "Is that your shovel?"

He frowned, glancing at it. "No. Somebody must've put it there."

He started to reach for it, but Aggie held out her arm, blocking him. "Why would someone do that?"

He looked at her impatiently. "I don't know. Wrong truck, I guess. You know, this really is starting to turn into harassment. Do I need to get a lawyer out here?"

Aggie said, "Did you happen to stop by the Shipwreck bait and tackle store yesterday morning around 6:00 a. m. and purchase a pack of fishing line?"

He threw up his hands in angry exasperation. "Okay, that's it. For your information, I did buy fishing line, which is one of the things people might reasonably be expected to do at the beach. And I'm also finished answering your lame-ass questions. Have a good day, Officer."

He swung toward the driver's door and Aggie caught his arm in a firm grip. He stared at her fingers on his muscled forearm incredulously.

"Chief," she said. "It's *Chief* Malone. And to answer your question, yes, you probably need to get a lawyer." She reached for her handcuffs. "Put your hands behind your back, please. You're under arrest for possession of stolen goods and impeding a homicide investigation."

CHAPTER
EIGHTEEN

D espite the extensive renovations, the Dogleg Island Police Station did not have a holding cell, mostly due to the objections of the other tenants who did not care to share their space with criminals. All arrests made on the island were sent across the bridge to the county detention center for booking. Aggie called Mo to finish the interviews at the campsite while Aggie completed the paperwork on Cade's arrest. A deputy arrived to transport Cade within half an hour, and Aggie turned over both the shovel and her prisoner to him gladly. Cade left still shouting threats and accusations of police harassment, promising to sue and bring charges of civil rights violations. Sally Ann looked mildly alarmed, but Aggie just shrugged.

"Wouldn't be the first time," she said, turning to go back into her office.

Jess Krieger came in the door just as the deputy was escorting the still-combative Cade out of the building. He nodded back over his shoulder. "Got yourself a live one, huh, Chief?" He took out his notebook. "What's the scoop?"

"Ongoing case, Jess," she responded, almost by rote. "No comment."

Jess Krieger was tall, lanky, sixtyish, and a giant pain in the ass, although perhaps not as much now as he once had been. He had retired as a prize-winning journalist from the *Miami Herald* to take over Dogleg Island's weekly newspaper, which at that time had consisted mostly of recipes and fishing forecasts, with the occasional wedding and birth announcements for color. Jess still printed the birth and wedding announcements, but he couldn't quite let go of his journalistic instincts. Whereas most community papers reported only the sanitized version of local crimes, usually doing nothing more than paraphrasing the deliberately bland press releases from the police department, Jess Krieger left no stone unturned in his determination to uncover— and print—the whole truth. Unfortunately, that truth was not always ready for public consumption, which was only one of the reasons for Aggie's antipathy for him.

Jess had won yet another award for his not-particularly-flattering coverage of the shooting incident that almost cost Aggie her life and the subsequent scandal that rocked the Murphy County Sheriff's Office. Aggie was a strong supporter of the

First Amendment, but she had never entirely trusted Jess after that. Her attitude toward him softened after his surprisingly compassionate and sensitive coverage of the War of Dogleg Island was picked up by the national press, but her relationship with him was still guarded.

"Wasn't that one of those kids from the demonstration at Beachside Park?" Jess persisted, following Aggie into her office.

Aggie glanced up from texting Grady. "What makes you think that?"

"I got pictures. Front page, below the fold."

Aggie texted Grady: *Package on the way. Make it a rush job, okay?*

To which her husband replied, *Anything for you, Chief.*

Aggie put her phone away and said to Jess, "Send me a copy, will you?"

"What for?"

"Professional courtesy." She sank into her desk chair and slid open the top drawer, searching for more ginger candies. Nothing but some pens, the wrinkled flyer Cade Rodan had thrust on her, and that beaded hair tie she had found in Geraldine Kidd's record room yesterday.

Jess made himself comfortable on the love seat and took out his phone. Flash, who considered the arrest of Cade Rodan a job well done and had already settled into his spot by the window while Aggie completed the inevitable paperwork, came over to greet him. Flash did not share Aggie's wary opinion of the reporter, who had never been anything but nice to him. The truth was, Flash liked most people, even those who didn't always remember to bring him a jerky treat when they visited.

Jess gave Flash a hearty rubdown, found a jerky treat in his pocket, and turned his attention to his phone while Flash took the treat to his dog bed to enjoy. "There," said Jess, hitting a key on his phone. "Photos sent. One good turn deserves another."

Aggie looked at him suspiciously. "Oh, yeah?"

He put his phone away and took up his pen and notebook again. "What can you tell me about the break-in at the historical society yesterday?"

"Absolutely nothing," replied Aggie. "Ongoing case."

"Anyone injured besides Grace Henderson?"

"No."

"Any suspects?"

"No."

"Can you confirm that the only items taken were some old survey maps from the eighties?"

Aggie stared at him. "Where did you hear that?"

"Nora Billings," he replied. "She took inventory after the break-in."

Aggie picked up the phone and punched the intercom button. "Sally Ann, get me Nora Billings on the phone."

"Yes, ma'am," Sally Ann replied. "Did you see the message from her on your desk?"

Aggie pushed aside the papers on her desk until she found the pink note from Sally Ann. It read:

From: Nora Billings
RE: Info you requested
Completed inventory. The only items missing are two survey maps commissioned in 1984 by Mercury Oil Co. Available to talk further after 1:00 p. m. Home phone…

Aggie said, "Never mind, Sally Ann. Thanks."

She put down the receiver and looked at Jess thoughtfully. "What can you tell me about the building of Mercury Park?"

Jess made a few notes on his pad. "I'm going to take that as a confirmation."

Aggie said, "I understand the current location wasn't the first choice. I saw a picture of it from 1983 that wasn't anywhere near the beach. Salty said the first site was shut down. He thought it had something to do with the government."

"I guess you could say that." Jess finished writing and looked up. "I wasn't here then, you understand, but I recall reading that when they started excavating the old site, they uncovered artillery shells, some of them unexploded."

Aggie's brows flew up. "What?"

Flash, having finished his treat, looked up with interest. He knew about the buried treasure on Dogleg, of course, and had even helped uncover some of it once, although that had turned out not to be the kind of treasure worth keeping. But why would someone want to bury things that exploded?

"The military used to use the island for target practice during World War Two," Jess explained.

"They'd fire their big guns from boats and planes to try to see what they could hit, I guess."

Now Aggie remembered Pete saying something about that in his speech yesterday. But he had definitely not mentioned unexploded artillery.

"Anyway," Jess went on, "the military came in, started doing underground surveys, found a bunch of that crap. They closed down the site, bought the land from Mercury, and cleaned it up the best they could."

"What do you mean, the best they could?"

He shrugged. "It's an island. Earth shifts. Some of the stuff that was too deep for them to find back then started coming up to the surface about ten years back. That would be before you came, but I was here for that story. Homeowner was clearing a spot for his greenhouse and uncovered a two-foot-long shell he dug out of the weeds. He didn't want his picture taken, but I got a shot of the ordnance. Front page."

"Good God," Aggie said.

"It was a dud," Jess assured her, "but the military confiscated it anyway. The point being, who knows how much more of that stuff is out there?"

"Huh," Aggie said.

Flash, watching her, could tell she was trying to put together a pattern in her head. That was the kind of thing she did even better than he did, and when she got that look on her face, he knew it wouldn't be long until the case was solved.

Except he thought the case was already solved with the arrest of Cade Rodan.

Jess tucked his notebook back in his pocket

and stood. "So when are you going to have some information on the break-in?"

Which one? Aggie thought, but she said, "Friday afternoon police reports, as usual."

"And the arrest of that protestor?"

"Same."

"Too late for this week's edition," he remarked.

She said, "Thanks for dropping by, Jess."

She stood and walked him to the door, Flash at her side. When he was gone, she turned to Sally Ann. "Do you know those ginger candies of Mo's?"

Sally Ann reached into a drawer and produced a bag. "She left these for you."

"Thank you," Aggie replied fervently, and tore open the bag.

Flash's ears pricked forward, even though he knew the candy wasn't for him and he didn't even particularly like the smell. But the crinkling of a cellophane bag was one of his favorite sounds, and he really couldn't help paying attention when he heard it.

"Chief, I think I've found a good candidate for office manager," Sally Ann said. "Lives in Ocean City, but she was raised here on Dogleg. She has kids in school but has family for childcare after school and on holidays. Good computer skills, office experience—managed her husband's business before she had children—used to be a 911 dispatcher so she knows the system, and her brother is a cop. Clean background check. And get this," she finished proudly, "her hobby is listening to true crime podcasts! I mean, she's practically in the business already."

Aggie tried not to roll her eyes at this but wasn't entirely successful. "I'm not sure I'd go that far," she said, "but she does sound good. I say get her in here, put her through her paces."

Sally Ann looked pleased. "Yes, ma'am, she's coming in this afternoon. I want to test her on the phone and our software before you interview her."

Aggie unwrapped a candy and popped it into her mouth. "Great. If you like her, leave her resume on my desk and set up an interview for tomorrow morning."

Sally Ann smiled broadly. "Thanks, Chief."

"Sally Ann, I'm sorry I gave you such a hard time before," Aggie began.

But Sally Ann was looking over Aggie's shoulder, a courteous, professional expression on her face. "May I help you, sir?"

Aggie turned to look at the man who had just come in. So did Flash, and he felt an immediate prickle of alert recognition in the ends of his fur.

Imagine that. It was the man in the green-checked shirt.

CHAPTER NINETEEN

He was no longer wearing the green-checked shirt, Flash noticed, but it was definitely the same man, the same leather messenger bag, and the same ponytail banded in three places. Flash, curious, started to move forward for a closer examination, but thought better of it. Aggie said some people didn't like dogs, which made absolutely no sense to Flash, and that he should always wait until he received some kind of indication that he was welcome before approaching a stranger. This man gave no such sign.

The man ignored Sally Ann and looked at Aggie. "Are you the police chief?"

Aggie replied, "That's right. I'm Chief Malone."

He came forward with his hand extended. "My name is Aaron Fisher. I understand you brought in one of our people this morning. Cade Rodan."

"That's right." She shook his hand, looking him over, and gestured to her office. "Come in and have a seat."

Aggie went behind her desk, gesturing for her guest to take a seat in the straight-backed chair in front of it. "Are you Mr. Rodan's lawyer?"

Aaron Fisher sat down in the chair she had indicated. Flash sat a few feet away from him, watching him alertly. "No," he replied with a small smile. "I just heard what happened and came down to see if I could be of help. I'm prepared to post bond if necessary." He reached for the clasp of his messenger bag.

Aggie held up a staying hand as she sat down. "I'm afraid Mr. Rodan is no longer here."

"He's been released, then?"

"No," replied Aggie. "He's been transferred to the Ocean City detention center for processing." She slid open her top drawer and tucked the bag of candy inside, at the same time slipping the beaded hair elastic out and into her pocket.

A small line appeared between his brows. "I don't understand. I thought he was brought in on a minor charge—shoplifting or something."

"I'm afraid it's more complicated than that." Aggie looked at him curiously. "You look familiar to me. Have you been here before?"

He gave an impatient shake of his head as he refastened the clasp of his bag and prepared to rise. "I'm sure we've never met."

Aggie said, "Maybe I saw you with the others at the

demonstration at Beachside Park yesterday."

He gave her a mildly condescending look. "I don't do demonstrations. I'm a journalist, doing interviews for my podcast on activists and social change."

Aggie knew this, of course, since Cade had given her Aaron Fisher's name barely an hour ago. She said, "It's generous of you to offer to pay Mr. Rodan's bond, especially since you're not really affiliated with the group."

He replied impatiently, "Could you tell me where this jail is? I'm not from around here."

"Go across the bridge, turn right, you'll see the signs after about a mile."

"Thank you."

Flash looked at Aggie curiously as she let the man walk toward the door, but then she stood up. "Excuse me," she said.

She came around the desk, holding out the green beaded hair elastic. "Is this yours?"

He took it from her. "Oh. Yes, thank you."

"You're sure?" she insisted as he turned again to go. "Because I found it yesterday, in the county records room after someone had jimmied the lock to get in."

He turned slowly, and his stiff smile did not quite hide the flicker of unease in his eyes. "Then I must be mistaken," he said. "It just looks like one of mine." He offered the hair tie in his open hand.

"I also remember where I've seen you before," Aggie said, ignoring his hand. "On the security footage from yesterday morning. You entered the building around eight o'clock, before any of the administrative offices were open, and you left half an hour later."

"I'm sure I don't—" he began.

Aggie cut him off. "Please sit down, Mr. Fisher," she said. "Let's talk."

There was a slight flaring of his nostrils and one shoulder turned slightly toward the door. Before he could exhale a breath or take a step Flash was between him and the door. Fisher took a startled step backwards, staring at Flash. Flash, shoulders crouched, held his gaze.

Aggie smiled and gestured toward the chair he had just left. After a moment, he took it.

Aggie returned to her own desk chair. Fisher crossed his legs and leaned back in his chair, doing his best to appear relaxed and cooperative. Flash stretched out in front of the door just in case he wasn't as cooperative as he appeared.

"So, Chief," Fisher said pleasantly. "What can I help you with?"

Aggie said, "What were you doing here yesterday morning?"

He replied easily, "I was here to do some research."

"What kind of research?"

"Property records," he answered.

"From 1979 through 1980?" Aggie suggested.

He just smiled. "When I came by there seemed to be some sort of event going on in the police station, and no one was in the records office. The door was open, so I went inside and waited a while. When no one came, I went into the file room to see if I could find what I needed myself. That's probably when I dropped this." He held up the hair tie with a wry smile.

"Did you find what you were looking for?" Aggie asked.

"I'm afraid not," he replied in that same casual tone. "I didn't have time to wait for someone to help me, so I decided to come back today. Unfortunately, this misunderstanding with Cade Rodan got in the way."

Aggie nodded. "Was the key in the lock of the file room when you went in?"

He looked regretful. "I'm afraid I didn't notice."

Aggie regarded him steadily. "Breaking into a public office is a criminal offense."

"That doesn't surprise me in the least." He glanced at his watch.

"And stealing public records can, under certain circumstances, rise to the level of a felony."

He looked unconcerned. "I doubt that very much."

"So my question is," Aggie went on mildly, "what could you possibly have been looking for that was worth risking a criminal charge for?"

"I have no idea what criminal charge you're talking about," he replied, exasperated. "I already told you what happened. Now, if you'll excuse me, I do have more pressing matters to attend to."

He started to rise, but Aggie made a firm downward motion with her hand. Reluctantly, he sank back into his seat. But instead of addressing him, Aggie picked up the phone and dialed a three-digit number.

"Geraldine," she said in a moment. "This is Chief Malone. Will you do me a favor and check the file room? See if those property file folders for 1979 and 1980 are there. Yes, I know, but check anyway, will you? I'll wait."

Fisher clenched his hands tensely against his thighs. Aggie smiled. "Can I have someone bring you a cup of coffee?"

He said shortly, "Chief Malone, I don't have time…"

But Aggie's attention turned back to the phone. She listened for a moment, then said, "Okay, Geraldine, thanks. One more thing. What time do you take your break?" As she listened to the answer, she held her visitor's gaze. "All right, thanks again," she said. "Have a good day."

She replaced the receiver and leaned back in her chair. "So," she said, "here's my theory. You broke into the records office yesterday morning…" At his sharp intake of breath, she raised a cautionary finger and continued, "Either because you didn't want to sign in and show ID, or because you were too impatient to wait. You left with the property deed files for 1979 and 1980. Having had twenty-four hours to study them—or copy them—you slipped them back into their proper place while Geraldine was on break, twenty minutes ago. Then you came in here on the pretense of offering to pay Mr. Rodan's bond in case anyone questioned what you were doing in the building. So my only remaining question," she concluded, watching him, "is the one I asked before. What were you looking for?"

He pressed his lips together briefly, and then, with a one-shouldered shrug, let out a breath. "What the hell," he said, sitting back. "I already told you I was here yesterday to do research. Despite your BS theory —which is completely unprovable, by the way—I've got nothing to hide."

"Good," Aggie said pleasantly, palms open. "So let's hear what you're not hiding."

He exhaled, long and slow, and settled back in his chair. "I told you my podcast is about activists. These guys..." He made a vague gesture toward the window. "They're just background. The stories I tell are about the real badasses—the Patty Hearsts, the Ceasar Chavez, the Malcolm Xs—along with some you never heard of. One of them, a fellow by the name of Richard Dunhill, is rumored to live right here on Dogleg Island. That's why I'm really here. To interview him."

Aggie scribbled down the name. "That doesn't sound familiar."

"It wouldn't," he said. His body language altered subtly as he warmed to his subject—leaning forward slightly, clasping his hands, relaxing his jaw. "In 1979 he turned state's evidence against his crew, the Red Rovers, and went into the witness protection program. New name, new identity, the works. That's how he ended up here."

Aggie was skeptical. "Dogleg Island isn't a very likely place for witness relocation."

"It was part of the deal," he replied confidently.

"How do you know this?"

"Some of his old gang are still alive," Fisher replied,

"doing life while he gets away with murder—literally. I interviewed them, got some insight."

Aggie was thoughtful. "You don't have his name, you don't have his address, you don't have a description, and you're not even one hundred percent sure he lives on Dogleg. So how, exactly, were you planning to interview him?"

"Part of the witness relocation deal is a house and a yearly stipend," Fisher replied. "Back in the eighties, before the bridge was built, this island was barely settled. I figured there couldn't be that many people buying houses—or building them, for that matter—during the time period I'm looking at. I just had to narrow it down."

"And did you find what you were looking for?"

He smiled. "Nice try, Chief. In fact, I've spent so much time talking to you I'm going to have to put my research on hold for yet another day." He stood up. "I assume we're finished?"

He turned toward the door, which Flash was still blocking, and glanced back at her. "Do you mind?"

Aggie beckoned Flash with her index finger and he responded immediately, sweeping across the room to sit at her side.

Aaron Fisher gave her a curt nod. "Have a good day, Chief."

CHAPTER
TWENTY

Aggie's search for "Richard Dunhill + Red Rovers" produced such a wealth of information that she felt she should be embarrassed for not having heard of them before. The Red Rovers, she learned, had been designated a domestic terrorist organization in the late 70s, operating mainly in the Midwest, but occasionally reaching as far south as Florida and Alabama. Their manifesto was a rant against rampant capitalism, and they emphasized their point by blowing up corporate offices. Dunhill, a disenchanted Vietnam veteran, was their explosives expert, having been trained in the field by the very government that was chasing him down.

Fourteen deaths were attributed to the Red Rovers in the five years of their peak operation. By 1979, only four of them were left: Richard Dunhill, Karen

Little, Mark Sheldon, and Nick Olson. They had lost none of their efficiency for their small numbers, however, financing themselves with bold robberies and dramatic escapes. The FBI moved in on them an hour before what was to be their grandest display of violence yet: the bombing of the Mercury Oil southeastern headquarters in Tallahassee. Nick Olson was killed in the shootout, Karen Little—who was pregnant at the time—and Mark Sheldon went to prison for life. Richard Dunhill, who, it was later revealed, was responsible for the tip that led to the apprehension of the other three, gave testimony against them and entered the witness protection program where, as far as Aggie could tell, he remained.

"Mercury Oil," she murmured at last, frowning as she sat back from the computer. "What are the odds?"

Flash looked up at her curiously, and she said, "No such thing as coincidence, Flash. Everybody knows that."

She dialed Geraldine's number again. "Geraldine," she said when the other woman answered, "Aggie Malone again. Will you pull those property records files from 1979 and '80 for me? I'll come down and get them."

"Honestly, Chief," she said, agitated, "I'm at a complete loss. I'm meticulous with those files, just meticulous. I swear they were missing yesterday, and then this morning they're back again? I just don't know what happened."

"That's okay," Aggie assured her, "I do." Then she

added, "No one's been in there since I talked to you, right?"

"No, ma'am," she replied righteously, "and I haven't left my desk."

"Okay," Aggie said, "I'll be there in a minute."

Aggie stood up and braced herself against a prickle of light-headedness. It was definitely time to seek out something to eat. The ginger candies were quelling the nausea, but they left a great deal to be desired in terms of nutrition.

She went into the outer office, saying, "Sally Ann, do you have any snacks in your..."

She broke off when she saw her sister-in-law, Lucy, sitting in Sally Ann's chair. Lucy was dressed in a lightweight pink suit, her dark hair neatly done up in a bun, makeup meticulously applied. She had lost weight since her divorce and no longer dressed like she spent her days eating toaster pastries and watching game shows on television. Today she looked particularly professional. Sally Ann, who was standing over Lucy's shoulder showing her something on the computer screen, looked around when Aggie spoke.

"Lucy," Aggie said, unable to hide her surprise. "What are you doing here?"

Flash paused in mid-step, looking around warily for the twins. He had nothing against Lucy, per se, but her boys were a menace. Flash generally found it best to be elsewhere when they were around.

Lucy said, "I'm applying for the job." She reached into her oversized mom-purse and brought out a protein bar, which she offered to Aggie. "Always carry a couple of these with you. Your blood sugar can drop like a stone before you know it." She said this with a note of disapproval, as though any fool should have known that.

Aggie took a hesitant step forward to accept the protein bar. "Oh. Um, thanks." She thought quickly. "Listen, Lucy, I'm glad you came in and I'm sure you'd be great at the job but I'm going to have to check the city's policy on nepotism..."

"I already checked," Sally Ann assured her. "There isn't one."

"Oh," Aggie said. "That's good." She widened her eyes meaningfully to Sally Ann, who made a point of pretending not to understand. Aggie said deliberately, "Sally Ann, I need you to help me with something in my office. Excuse us a minute, Lucy. And, um..." She held up the protein bar. "Thanks."

Sally Ann told Lucy, "Okay, the phones are yours. Remember—name, address, phone number, time, and nature of complaint. If anything comes in from dispatch, I'll answer it. You can practice filling in a log sheet until I get back."

Lucy waved her away. "Got it."

Aggie ushered Sally Ann into her office. Flash followed hurriedly. Aggie closed the door and leaned against it, saying, "No. No, no, no, *no*."

"She's the best candidate we've had," Sally Ann objected quickly. "She picked up the filing system and software programs in five minutes. She was a 911 dispatcher and knows all the protocols. She already knows how to operate the radio. Her husband has her children three days a week and they're in an after-school program the rest of the time. Her next-door neighbor is available for emergency babysitting. She types faster than I do." She paused long enough to draw a breath. "You're not going to find anyone more qualified. I can have her ready to take over by Monday."

Aggie was still shaking her head. Flash watched balefully. "She's my sister-in-law. I can't have her working for me. It's a recipe for disaster."

"You said," Sally Ann reminded her stubbornly, "it was my decision."

"Yes, but..."

"Just look at her resume," Sally Ann insisted. "Interview her like you would anyone else. If you can find anything legitimately wrong with her..." She emphasized the word "legitimately" slightly, "then, well, you have the final decision. Fair enough?"

"Well," said Aggie.

"And..." Sally Ann turned on her heel to leave, "the clock is ticking."

Aggie stepped away from the door and watched her leave without a reply. When she was gone, she tore open the protein bar and took a bite. It tasted like dust.

CHAPTER TWENTY-ONE

Mo called as Aggie was returning to her office with the property deed files in her hands.

"I talked to every one of them knuckleheads out at the campground," she reported, "except for the fellow in the camper. He took off before I could get to him. Not a one of them knows a thing, or so they claim. The camp hosts said they did hear somebody come in around 4:00 this morning, but said that's not unusual since the protestors moved in. A bunch of folks are already at the environmental center, putting up flags and banners and such for the grand opening this afternoon. You want me to hang around and make sure there's no trouble?"

If Aggie had had one more officer, the answer would have been simple. The park was currently a hot spot and having an officer on the scene from now until the rally this afternoon would definitely be an advantage. But while she and Mo had both been otherwise occupied, several minor complaints had come in that needed attention. She said reluctantly, "No, I guess not. Mr. Walker is complaining about the people in the rental next door blocking his driveway again, so you'd better go talk to them. And Bill Gray said he saw somebody creeping around his shed last night. If you'll take the report, I'll meet you back at the environmental center after lunch to help set up the traffic barriers. I want to make sure those demonstrators know exactly where they are and are not allowed to protest."

"Now, you know you've got no business working out in this sun moving traffic barriers," Mo scolded. "I'll get the camp hosts to do it."

"Jeez, Mo, you're as bad as Grady," Aggie said. She sat down at her desk and opened one of the folders. "I'll just supervise, okay? See you around 1:00."

She wasn't entirely sure what she was looking for, but she was sure that if Aaron Fisher thought there was something of importance in these folders it was worth taking a look. From what she had read, Richard Dunhill was twenty-eight when he had gone into witness protection some time toward the end of 1979 or early 1980. He had no family. So she was looking for a property deed in the name of a single man with no co-owners and no mortgage. The problem was that in the late seventies virtually all property was registered in the name of a man, whether or not he was married, and property on Dogleg was so cheap back then that a mortgage wasn't always necessary.

In the eighteen months between June of 1979, when the Red Rovers were apprehended, and December of 1980, less than two dozen properties had been purchased on Dogleg Island. Six were beach cottages, with the mortgages held by First United Bank of Murphy County. When she checked the addresses, she found four had since been resold, two had been destroyed by hurricanes and their lots reclaimed for back taxes. Eight lots had been purchased in what was now known as the Hidden Shores subdivision. Two were financed through banks or credit unions, and she marked them off her list. She painstakingly typed each of the remaining names into a search engine. One had died in 2015. Three others, in their fifties when they purchased the land, had died much earlier. The other two had sold their lots before ever building on them.

There were a handful of other deeds in the 1980's file, most of whom she knew. William Mitchell, Sally Ann's grandfather, who had established Island Real Estate in 1975, Obadiah Jessup from the Shipwreck Bait Shop, Lee Jennings, who owned an auto repair shop just across the bridge, a few others. She thought she could safely rule out Sally Ann's grandfather, who had been almost forty in 1980, and Mr. Obadiah, who had been born and raised on Dogleg. She put those aside and started examining the other deeds when Flash suddenly scrambled from his bed and raced toward the door. She looked up as Manny tapped lightly on the frame. "Excuse me, Chief Aggie." He grinned and dropped to one knee to greet Flash with a hearty chin rub. "Hello, Mr. Flash."

"Hi, Manny." Aggie closed the folder. "What brings you over this way?"

He got to his feet and held up a white paper sack with the Pete's Place logo on it. "Miss Lorraine said could I bring this to you on my way to class. Tuna fish sandwiches and fruit salad. It's early for lunch, but maybe you can keep it cold in your refrigerator?"

"It's never too early for lunch," Aggie assured him. She came around the desk to take the sack from him, peeking eagerly inside. "Manny, you're a lifesaver. And give Lorraine a big hug and kiss for me."

Manny grinned as he turned to go. "Maybe I'll just say you are happy."

Aggie looked up from examining the contents of the sack. "Manny, can you hold on just a minute?"

He started to object but she assured him, "It'll only take a sec, I promise."

She quickly grabbed her phone from her desk and brought up the photo Jess had sent her of the demonstrators. They were all gathered around a long picnic table at Mercury Park, and all the faces were clearly visible—especially Cade Rodan's. She showed the picture to Manny. "Can you tell me if any of these people is the one you saw giving money to River Keagan at Pete's Place Saturday night?"

He glanced at her curiously and she clarified, "River Keagan is the guy you saw in that photo I had yesterday."

He inclined his head, remembering, then took the phone from her. He studied the photo for only a minute, then said, "Yeah, sure, I see him. Here."

He turned the phone toward her, pointing toward the person sitting at the head of the table. It wasn't Cade Rodan. It was Aaron Fisher.

Aggie moved closer. "This one? You're sure?"

"It's the hair," he explained, pointing to Fisher's ponytail. "Three bands, you know. I never saw it done like that before on a white man. I remember."

Aggie took the phone from him, still looking at the photograph uneasily. "Thanks, Manny," she said, and even managed to give a quick smile. "Don't let me make you late for class."

When he was gone, Aggie returned to her desk and sat down heavily, her brow creased with troubled thought. She glanced at Flash, who was gazing hopefully at the lunch bag on the corner of her desk. "This," she told him, "changes everything."

At that moment her phone rang.

"Good news, good news, and bad news," Grady said when she answered.

"Good news first," Aggie said. "I need some."

"The blood on the shovel matches that of the vic," he replied. "Looks like we've got our murder weapon. Thanks for that."

"Thank Flash," she said, who pricked up his ears at the sound of his name.

"I intend to. Dog biscuits or pork chops?"

Flash, overhearing, pricked his ears even higher, and Aggie laughed softly. "What do you think?"

"Other good news," Grady went on, "Blood on the crowbar you took from the hardware store break-in also matches that of our victim, one River Keagan, deceased. Looks like he's the one who stole the shovel and the det cord. We know what happened to the shovel, but the only person who might tell us what he did with the det cord is, well, deceased."

"Is that the bad news?"

"Not entirely. The fingerprints on the shovel are *not* a match for those of Cade Rodan, who is at this minute pitching a temper fit in our holding cell. Neither are the ones you took from the historical society break-in. Looks like we've got the wrong guy if you're trying to tag him for the break-in or the murder."

Aggie let out a long breath, staring at the picture on her phone. "I know. It looks like I just let the right guy walk right out the door."

"Name?" Grady demanded.

"Aaron Fisher. Manny just identified him as the man who handed money to River Keagan Saturday night, I'm guessing as a down payment on stealing the det cord. I'm texting you a photo. There's a chance he might be headed your way to bail out Rodan. If he shows, hold him for questioning until I get there."

"Copy that, Chief. Anything else?"

"Yeah." She cast an uneasy glance toward her closed door. "Guess who's applying for Sally Ann's job?"

"Who?"

"Your sister." And into his incredulous silence she clarified, "Lucy."

"Don't do it, babe," he said firmly. "Listen to the

man who loves you. You're asking for nothing but trouble."

"I know," she agreed miserably. "But I don't know how to get out of it. Why didn't you tell me she was a 911 dispatcher?" There was a note of accusation in her voice with that.

"It was a long time ago," he replied defensively, "before she was married. Besides, it's not my fault. Who knew she was even looking for a job?"

"Great," she muttered. Then, "I'm sorry I fell asleep last night. Did you talk to Bishop?"

There was only a slight hesitance. "Yeah, just for a minute."

"What did you tell him?"

"That I'd think about it."

"So," she persisted, unwrapping one of the tuna sandwiches, "what are you thinking?"

"Ah, I don't know, babe." He sounded unhappy. "It's the best thing, I guess. I mean, I'm way more qualified than any of the other guys who are talking about running. We could use the money. I hate politicking, but I could probably win. I guess I'll do it."

Aggie said, "You don't have to make a decision this minute."

"Pretty soon, though."

"Sleep on it a couple of nights," she advised. "Meantime, how many deputies can you send me for the rally this afternoon?"

"I've got Higgins, Walters, and Sandford down."

Aggie chewed and swallowed the bite of sandwich she had taken. "Higgins," she said thoughtfully. "I like him. Do you suppose he'd be interested in a job at the beach?"

"Hardly," Grady replied. "He's got a wife, two kids, and one on the way. He can barely make it on the salary he has now."

"Well, tell him to contact me if he wants some off-duty work."

"Will do. What do you want to do with Cade Rodan?"

"Let him stew for a while," she replied. "Maybe having him in jail will cool the temperature on that rally this afternoon."

"Good thinking. Love you, babe. Stay out of the sun."

"You, too. See you tonight."

Aggie disconnected and returned to the file folder, munching on the tuna sandwich as she went through the remaining records. One by one she ruled out the names—wrong age, relatives and place of birth known to her, subject deceased—until there was only one name left.

It was the last one she had expected.

Aggie offered the rest of the sandwich to Flash, who accepted gratefully, and wiped her hands on a paper napkin. She typed the name into a law-enforcement database, hoping to find some evidence that he had existed before 1980. There was nothing.

Aggie went back through her search history and brought up the article on the Red Rovers. She stared at it for a long time.

Karen Little: Tulip

Mark Sheldon: Cappy

Nick Olson: Ziggy

Richard Dunhill: Rocketman

"Rocketman," she said softly. Flash looked up at her curiously.

Of course, she did not have any definitive proof. The whole purpose of witness protection was that the identity of the witness in question would be erased. Nonetheless, it looked as though Aaron Fisher was right: Richard Dunhill, the notorious eco-terrorist from the seventies, was alive and well and living on Dogleg Island. And Fisher, having stolen and examined the same files Aggie had just read, had come to the same conclusion.

The question was, what did he intend to do with that information?

Aggie exited the program and stood. "Come on, Flash," she said. "Let's go find Aaron Fisher."

Flash raced toward the door, but before he could reach it, Sally Ann opened the door without knocking. Her face was pale, her eyes big. She just stood there for a breath, seeming to search for words, and Aggie took a concerned step toward her.

"Chief," Sally Ann blurted. "There was this man. On the phone." She made a jerky motion over her shoulder. "You'd better come. He said there was a bomb."

CHAPTER TWENTY-TWO

E very incoming call to the Dogleg Island Police Department was recorded, along with the caller's number, if available. Aggie followed Sally Ann into the reception area, saying, "Play it back." Lucy watched anxiously but, for once, was silent. Aggie leaned over Sally Ann's shoulder and watched her tap a couple of keys on her computer. The caller ID came up as a blocked number. The message began to play.

The voice was male, muffled, and deepened in an amateurish way. Flash, sitting at Aggie's feet, recognized it immediately. Aggie was not so certain. It said: *Listen to me. There's a bomb in Mercury Park.* The last two words sounded staticky and blurred, but they were decipherable. *It's not our intention to waste human life. You have eighty-two minutes, starting now.*

Aggie looked at the time stamp on the incoming

call. Three minutes had already passed.

Lucy said, frowning, "I've heard that before."

"The voice?" Aggie demanded sharply.

"Maybe," she said uncertainly. "Or the words. Maybe both."

Aggie turned to Sally Ann, dismissing her. "Activate an alert. All units to Mercury Park. Get the bomb squad down here ASAP."

Before she finished speaking, Lucy swung her chair around to the radio and picked up the mic. "Dispatch, this is Dogleg Island Police. We have a bomb threat at Mercury Park, 128 Mercury Way. All units requested to assist with evacuation."

Sally Ann was already on the phone with the FDLE, requesting the bomb squad. Aggie headed for the door, punching Bishop's private number on her phone.

"Sending twelve units your way," he said when he answered. Bishop never took his ear from the radio and would have heard the call as soon as Lucy sent it out. "What else?"

"Cade Rodan," Aggie said, striding toward her vehicle, "in cuffs. He might not be behind this, but he knows who is."

"I'll bring him myself," Bishop said and disconnected.

Sally Ann called after her from the doorway, "Bomb squad is fifty minutes out."

Aggie lifted her hand in acknowledgement and opened the door for Flash. He jumped in just as the text came in from Grady. *Confidence?*

They had worked together long enough that

many of their conversations were in shorthand. He was asking what her confidence level was that this was a credible threat. It didn't make any technical difference, because they had to treat any bomb threat as though it was real, but she knew his concern was personal. She typed "6," then remembered Richard Dunhill. Rocketman. She changed it to "8."

Grady sent back, *4 minutes out.*

Aggie could already hear the chorus of sirens coming over the bridge.

Seven minutes later two sheriff's department cruisers were driving up and down the sandy roads of the park, announcing the emergency evacuation via megaphone. A team of deputies was assigned to clear out the campground, another to scout the trails. Aggie, Mo, and Grady swung their vehicles in front of the environmental center, with its domed roof glittering with solar panels. The wind whipped up dust devils of sand across the newly graded parking lot and snapped the American flag that hung in front of the building. Half a dozen people were working outside, and they looked around curiously when the three vehicles swung in front of the building, lights flashing and radios crackling loudly.

Two men were on a ladder, struggling against the wind to hang a banner over the front door. Several people moved around the building, sticking flags into the ground, while others set up a lectern and strung wire for the sound system. Mr. McMasters was spreading cedar mulch around a newly planted flower bed, gusts of wind bending back the brim of his straw hat. A handful of protestors had already gathered, holding signs that read, "You've Been Bought by Big Oil!" and "Dolphins Died for You!"

Aggie flipped the megaphone switch on her microphone. "Mercury Park is under an emergency evacuation order. Please make your way in an orderly fashion to the exit. Do not stop to collect your belongings. Repeat, the park is closed. This is an emergency evacuation. You are ordered to leave the park immediately. Do not panic. Make your way to the exit in an orderly fashion."

Flash, watching from his seat in the SUV, couldn't help wondering over how very slow to understand people could be. Most of them simply looked around in confusion at Aggie's amplified words, conferred among themselves, or went back to what they were doing. Flash didn't like to judge, but even he knew what the word "emergency" meant. And couldn't they smell the tension in the air? Only Mr. McMasters, who was tucking mulch around a low bush with purple flowers, stood up and took off his gloves, moving toward the parking lot.

Grady and Mo got out of their vehicles and Flash sprang out to join them. He arrived as Grady was saying loudly, "Okay, folks, this is not a drill. Clear this area."

Mo strode forward, declaring, "What's the matter with you people? You deaf? Get in your cars, get out of this park! That's a police order!"

There was a clamor of, "What's going on?" and "You can't close the park! We have an event!" From the protestors came the expected cries of, "Police harassment!" and "First Amendment!"

Flash got into his crouch and emitted several short, sharp barks, which got most people's attention. Grady took one man by the shoulder and turned him politely but firmly toward the parking lot. *"Now*, sir. No, leave your flags. Go straight to the exit." He took another woman's arm and repeated, "Now. Go directly to the exit."

One by one and group by group, calmly but hurriedly, Grady ushered people toward their cars. When one of the sunburned protestors started chanting, "Stand your ground! Stand your ground!" Mo grabbed the sign from him and got in his face. "I'll show you what ground you can stand on, punk, and it's right outside the gate! Get moving!"

Aggie called, "Is anyone in the building?"

Mo went up the steps and shouted to the two people on ladders who were stringing the banner over the door, "Y'all want me to come up and get you? Get down off of there!" She moved past them and checked the door. "Door's locked, Chief!"

Aggie started toward the building, calling back, "Check the back!" Her phone rang. She glanced at it, but rejected the call when she saw it was Lucy. Bishop's car pulled up behind hers and she turned to meet him. Flash, seeing that Grady had the situation well in hand, trotted over to join her.

Bishop got out and leaned on his open door,

squinting in the sun. "How much time?"

"Sixty-two minutes," she replied. "If the caller was telling the truth, the bomb squad should get here just in time to get their robots blown up."

"That's what the taxpayers bought them for," Bishop replied. "You think this has something to do with the protest this afternoon?"

"One hundred percent," she replied. She nodded toward the back of his car. "Did you bring Rodan?"

"He's all yours." Bishop opened the back door, reached inside, and pulled Cade Rodan out by the arm.

"What the hell?" demanded Cade as soon as he was on his feet. His hands were cuffed in front of him, and he was wearing a shapeless county-issued cotton shirt over the board shorts in which Aggie had arrested him. Despite his belligerence, he looked slightly less confident than he had a few hours ago.

He glared at Aggie. "My uncle is on the way down here, you know. He's going to have this Podunk police department for breakfast."

Aggie's phone rang again. Lucy. Impatiently, she dismissed it. She said to Cade, "We have information that there's a bomb somewhere in this park. Tell me what you know, and I unlock those cuffs right now and your uncle will have wasted a trip. Keep quiet and you're going to federal prison for twenty-five years to life. What will it be?"

"What makes you think I know anything about a bomb?" he shot back. But there was a flicker of uneasiness in his eyes that told Aggie all she needed to know.

Grady, having successfully urged the bystanders to their cars, came over and stood a few feet away, his hands on his gun belt. Including Flash, Cade Rodan was surrounded by four police officers, all of them with eyes hard on him, all of them silent, waiting for him to speak.

Aggie said, "Did you steal, or tell anyone else to steal, a reel of detonation cord from Keller's Hardware yesterday?"

His brows drew together in a quick, shocked frown. "What? No. I didn't steal anything."

Flash glanced at Aggie. He could tell she believed him. So did Flash.

Aggie said, "What was the fishing line for? And don't bother lying. You didn't have any fishing equipment in your gear."

Cade sucked in a breath through his nostrils, hesitated, and said, "I don't know. Fisher, the podcast dude, ask me to pick it up as long as I was going surfing on the north side of the island yesterday morning." He paused, took another breath, then seemed to come to a decision. "When I dropped it by his place, I guess I surprised him. He had some papers spread out on a table, like diagrams or maps or something, and he tried to hide them. Maybe they were plans, I couldn't see."

Aggie said sharply, "Plans for what?"

He shrugged awkwardly, trying to stretch out his hands in the cuffs. "I don't know. Maybe nothing. Probably nothing. It's just that... there was a bag of fertilizer on the floor next to the table. Not something you expect to see when a guy's living out of a camper, you know? So I kind of joked, 'What are you doing, man, making a bomb?' And he got all weird-like, saying what the hell do I know about it anyway and maybe I should just mind my own business, so I told him to chill and got the hell out of there. Shit, I barely know the guy, what was I supposed to do? I didn't think anything else about it until you said something about explosives this morning, and that's the truth."

Aggie glanced at Bishop, then at Grady. Their faces were grim.

"Do you think Fisher was planning to set off a bomb as part of the demonstration this afternoon?" she said to Cade.

He shook his head helplessly. "Why would he? He's not even with the group."

She insisted, "Did you ever hear him say anything that might give a hint as to where he would plant a bomb, if there was one? Think."

Again he shook his head. "That's all I know, swear to God. Listen..." he glanced around anxiously. "Do you think he really did it? Is there a bomb somewhere?"

Aggie hesitated only another moment, then she took out a key and unlocked his handcuffs. "You'll receive a summons in the mail to appear on the pending charges. Meantime, you're free to go. Get a ride with one of your friends and get out of here."

He took a hurried step forward and then glanced back, rubbing his wrists. "My truck..."

"No time," Aggie said sharply. "Just go!"

He jogged toward the line of cars that were making their way out of the park, found one he recognized, and flagged down a ride. Mo came up just as he left. "Building's locked up," she reported. "I didn't see anybody else."

"This is the most likely location," Grady put forth, "if the bomb is related to the demonstration. Shouldn't we have a look inside?"

Bishop gave a sharp shake of his head. "Not our job. We're not equipped or qualified. We wait for the bomb squad."

Aggie's phone rang again, and this time it was the office. "Sally Ann," she said, trying not to sound impatient, "what is it?"

But it was not Sally Ann who replied. "Aggie, this is Lucy. Listen, I..."

"Oh, for God's sake, Lucy," Aggie returned impatiently, "this is a police line!"

She started to disconnect, but Lucy rushed on, "I remembered where I'd heard it before. The bomb threat. Listen to this."

There was some rustling and a muffled thump, and then the voice Aggie had heard less than half an hour ago, saying the same words. Or almost the same. *Listen to me. There's a bomb in the Mercury Oil Building. It's not our intention to waste human life. You have eighty-two minutes, starting now.*

Aggie's attention quickened. He'd changed the words: "Mercury Oil Building" to "Mercury Park." She remembered an anomaly in the phone call, how the words "Mercury Park" had been staticky and muffled, even a slightly different tenor than the rest of the statement. That was because it was a recording, and it had been edited.

She said, "Lucy..."

But the recording wasn't over. Another voice spoke, younger, clearer, and very familiar: *That was the phone call Richard Dunhill made to the police on the morning of what was meant to be the Red Rovers' most dramatic display of violence yet. Other such phone calls had been made to other police districts in the past, but this one was actually a signal, prearranged between Dunhill and law enforcement, to let the FBI know it was safe to move in. Five minutes after making that call, Richard Dunhill walked out of the Mercury Oil Building and into the protective custody of the FBI, which immediately swarmed the building with guns blazing. One member of the Red Rovers, Nick Olson—also known as Ziggy— was killed in the shoot-out, and the remaining two taken into custody. The bomb, which Dunhill had defused before planting, was never denotated.*

Today we'll be talking to the last surviving member of the Red Rovers, who is currently serving a life sentence in the federal prison in Sumpterville, Florida, about the events of that day. This is Aaron Fisher, and you are listening to Episode Six of "World on Fire."

"It's a podcast," Lucy said, a little breathlessly. "That was the last episode I listened to. Do you think..."

Aggie interrupted urgently, "Lucy, play that again."

She pushed the speaker button on her phone and watched as Grady, Mo, and Bishop listened to what she had just heard. As soon as it finished, Aggie commanded, "Get Sally Ann on the phone."

"Okay," Lucy replied. "Do you want me to..."

Aggie said sharply, "I want you to put Sally Ann on the phone."

Without needing to be told, Sally Ann said, "I have the phone call from this morning cued up."

"Let's hear it."

When the call finished playing, Bishop muttered, "It's the same guy."

Aggie shook her head. "He used that clip for the phone call to the station," she said, "and edited in the words 'Mercury Park.'" She spoke into the phone again, "Sally Ann, I need you to find everything you can on Aaron Fisher and call me back. We're on a deadline," she reminded her just before she disconnected.

Bishop said harshly, "Are you telling me this whole thing is a stunt for his damn podcast?"

Aggie's brows knit together anxiously as she brought up the photo Jess had sent her, cropped and enlarged Aaron Fisher, and sent it to Bishop. "Maybe. But at this point I'd say that's the best-case scenario. I just sent you Fisher's photo."

"I'll put out a BOLO," he said, taking out his phone, "and make sure the deputies check everybody who goes through the gate on the way out."

"It's a podcast," Grady pointed out. "Anybody could have recorded it and edited in Mercury Park as a prank."

"A prank that'll get them prison time," Mo put in

shortly.

Aggie said, "I interviewed Aaron Fisher this morning. He seemed to think that terrorist, Dunhill, is living here on Dogleg."

A gust of wind flattened Grady's sun-bleached hair and then blew it back across his forehead. He frowned and pushed it back impatiently. "I don't recognize that name. Do you?" He looked from Bishop to Aggie.

"Witness protection," Aggie pointed out. "He'd have a different name."

"Not something the sheriff's office would be privy to," Bishop admitted.

Aggie's collar radio crackled with, "All clear from the campground." And in another moment, "Picnic grounds clear."

Aggie returned to her radio, "We're clear from the environmental center. Hiking trails?"

"Four evacuated from hiking trails. One half mile to clear."

Aggie said, "You've got thirty-eight minutes to clear the park. Make one more loop with the patrol announcements, and report to the front entrance."

Grady glanced at his watch. "Fourteen and a half minutes to clear the whole park. Not bad."

"Not out of the woods yet," Aggie reminded him worriedly.

Bishop said, "The bomb squad should be directed to the environmental center first, since that's the most likely trigger point. Your call," he added to Aggie with a quick apologetic glance.

"Yeah," agreed Aggie absently. She looked back

at the environmental center, its "Grand Opening" banner hanging crookedly by one nail and flapping in the wind. She looked down at Flash. She murmured, "Something's off. Something I'm missing."

"Babe," Grady said, "You've got the makings of a homemade bomb in the hands of an amateur who runs a podcast called 'World on Fire' and who's obsessed with violent activists. You've got a known ecoterrorist possibly living on the island, and a bomb threat. We follow procedure. Simple as that."

"Yeah," agreed Aggie, but her expression was still troubled. "Let's clear out. Mo, I need you to help with traffic control. Sheriff, as soon as we're sure the civilians are clear I'll need four or five men to help secure the perimeter until the bomb squad is finished searching."

"No problem," returned Bishop. And then he gave her an encouraging smile. "Hey, even if it does turn out to be a prank, we got in a good drill."

Aggie's phone rang. She answered it, listened for a moment, then put it away, turning to the others. "Okay, that's it. The bomb squad is here. Let's move out."

CHAPTER TWENTY-THREE

F lash watched in disappointment as the boxy white armored truck lumbered through the entrance to the park. Already drones were circling overhead, but Flash had seen drones before. What he had been looking forward to seeing were the robots that Aggie said would be deployed as soon as the truck reached the environmental center. He had never seen robots before, much less the kind that could disarm a bomb. He had hoped today would be the day.

After Aggie and Bishop briefed the bomb squad, they were all sent to wait outside the perimeter that was established twenty feet back from the entrance to the park. Evacuees had lined both sides of the road and a row of cars trying to get into the park for the afternoon's open house had formed behind them. Mo marched up and down the row of impatient drivers, telling them to hold their damn horses and lay off the horn, while deputies stationed themselves at intervals along the sides of the road where anxious evacuees were demanding to know what was going on. Once the bomb squad was deployed, there was nothing for Aggie and Flash to do but stay by the unit, monitoring the crackle of radio messages that went back and forth.

Grady came to stand beside them. "How're you holding up?" he asked Aggie.

She took a final drink from her water bottle. "I'm starving," she replied. "And…" She crumpled up the plastic bottle and tossed it in the back of the SUV. "I need to pee."

"Can't help with that," he replied, "But I brought gummy bears." He held out the bag to her.

She cast him an amused look and thrust her hand into the bag. "You carry gummy bears in your patrol car?"

"Don't you?" He popped one into his mouth and watched the truck disappear around the curve of the road as it moved toward the environmental center. "The bridge is closed to incoming traffic," he reported, "and every car that leaves is being searched for Fisher. I've got deputies going door to door looking for him. But," he added, "if he's already left the island we're falling behind. It could take hours for them to clear the park, assuming we don't all get blown to hell in the next twenty-two minutes, of course. Meantime, your suspect is getting God-knows how far away."

Aggie chewed a lime bear thoughtfully. "Yeah."

"My men searched the camper. No time to do a great job, but no sign of a bomb or plans to build one. All his stuff was there. They said it looked like he was planning to come back."

"Right," Aggie murmured. She ate a cherry bear.

"I could pull more men to search for Fisher," he said.

She responded only, "Hmm." She reached for more candy.

Grady held the bag away from her. "What are you thinking?"

Flash sometimes heard people say to Aggie, "Wouldn't you love to know what Flash is thinking?" which always struck him as odd, because Aggie always knew what he was thinking—just like he, most of the time, knew what she was thinking. Right now Flash was thinking about patterns, and how they never, ever failed. About locks that were broken for papers and locks that were broken for tools. About voices from the past and voices from the present. And he thought, when he looked at her, that Aggie was too.

Also, as exciting as the morning had been and despite Flash's disappointment over the robots, he knew there were no explosives in the park. He thought Aggie knew that too.

Aggie said, "Det cord and fishing line. What does that make you think of?"

He frowned a little, putting it together. "Some kind of remote-control device?" Then, eyes narrowing, "No. A trip wire."

She nodded and reached for the bag of gummy

bears again. "My thoughts exactly. But the phone call made it sound like a time bomb, or even a manually detonated one."

"Yeah," Grady pointed out,"but it was a recording of another bomb threat that might not have anything to do with this one—if there even is a bomb this time."

Aggie's phone rang.

"Chief," said Sally Ann when she answered. Her voice sounded tense, although whether it was from excitement or anxiety Aggie couldn't tell. "I haven't finished researching Aaron Fisher yet, but Lucy told me something you need to know. That woman Fisher interviewed in prison for his last podcast? Her name is Karen Little, and like he said, she's the last surviving member of the Red Rovers if you don't count Richard Dunhill. She's also Aaron Fisher's mother."

Flash, watching as Aggie listened to Sally Ann, saw the pieces snap together in Aggie's eyes. The pattern was complete.

Aggie thanked Sally Ann and disconnected. She looked at Grady. "The bomb isn't here." She spoke softly, almost under her breath, as though thinking the words through even as she spoke them. "This is just a decoy. The real bomb is at the old site."

Grady frowned, "The old site of what?"

"It wasn't plans for a bomb Rodan saw in Aaron Fisher's camper," Aggie said. "It was a map. Survey maps of the old Mercury Park site that he stole from the historical society. Whatever he's done, he did it there."

"Okay," Grady allowed cautiously. "But why?"

"Because," Aggie said, "that's where Richard Dunhill is."

Before he could speak, she rushed on, "Aaron Fisher has got nothing against Mercury Oil. That's not why he came here. He came here for Richard Dunhill. He came for the man who betrayed his mother and put her in prison for the past forty-five years. He came here for revenge."

Flash hurried around to the passenger side of the vehicle and jumped in through the open window, taking his seat.

Grady said, "Wait. Didn't you tell me Dunhill is in witness protection? Even if he is here on the island, Fisher doesn't know how to find him. And neither do we."

Aggie opened her car door. "Yes," she said, "we do."

CHAPTER
TWENTY-FOUR

The narrow sand road wound deep into the undergrowth, crowded by tangled vines and broken pines, spike-leafed saw palmettos and bright flashes of bromeliads. After a quarter of a mile or so, the road, which was actually a driveway of sorts, forked at a chain-link fence. Aggie and Flash turned left; Grady, in the vehicle behind them, turned right.

Aggie could see glimpses of plastic-covered hoop houses and potting sheds beyond the fence, and, eventually, the slope of the cedar-shingled roof that covered the one-room cottage. She drew up in front of the closed gate and parked next to a white truck with landscaping supplies in the back and a rocket logo painted on the side panel. The words "Rocket Landscaping & Design" arched over the graphic. "Flash," she said quietly, staring at the scene in front of her. "Wait."

Flash had no intention of doing otherwise.

The cottage was square and covered with wood siding, blending so perfectly into its surroundings it was almost camouflaged. The unpainted door was flanked on either side by an enormous banana tree, and a curved, shell-lined flower bed followed the flow of a walkway made of polished concrete and bottle-glass stepping stones. The neatly mulched yard was decorated with brightly painted terracotta pots that held blooming wildflowers and purple pampas grass. In the center of that yard sat Aaron Fisher, strapped to a lawn chair with yellow det cord. His hands and feet were tied with gardening wire and there was a strip of tape over his mouth. He looked, understandably, terrified. In a second lawn chair a few feet away sat Mason McMasters, a shotgun across his knees.

Aggie pushed the button on her collar radio and quietly described the situation to Grady.

He replied, "Eyes on a black Ranger parked at the edge of the field where the original park was sited. No occupants. Tag comes back to Aaron Fisher. I'm calling for backup and approaching your location on foot from the west."

Aggie said, "Be careful. And keep this channel open."

"Copy that."

Aggie put her hand on her weapon and got slowly out of her car, standing beside the door. Flash came to stand beside her, eyes and ears alert, muscles tense. Mason McMasters watched them with a pleasant, vaguely approving expression on his face.

"Good for you, Miss Chief," he said. "I wasn't sure you'd figure it out. But just in case you did..." He gestured with the shotgun toward Fisher. "I held on to your prize for you."

Aggie said, "What's going on, Mr. McMasters?"

The corners of his lips deepened into his weathered face with a very small smile. "Well now," he said, "I think you know that's not my real name. But I appreciate the courtesy all the same."

"Mr. Dunhill, then," Aggie said. She nodded toward Aaron Fisher, her hands on her gun belt. "What happened here?"

He replied, "I'll be glad to bring you up to speed on that, ma'am, but first I wonder if you'd satisfy my curiosity. How did you figure out who I was? I know how this degenerate did it." He nodded briefly toward Fisher. "But what gave me away to you?"

"It was nothing you did," Aggie assured him. "I never would have suspected anything if Mr. Fisher hadn't come looking. You paid cash for a lot next to the original site of Mercury Park in 1980. You were the right age. There's no record of you anywhere before you moved here. You wouldn't have your picture taken for the paper, despite all the work you did on the community center—the same way you wouldn't have your picture taken when you found that artillery shell on your property while you were building your greenhouse ten years ago. And of course..." She gestured backwards to his truck parked next to her vehicle. "There's Rocket Landscaping. I always did think it was a funny name. Also," she admitted, "there was something familiar about your voice, when I heard it played back on the podcast this morning. The average person wouldn't have noticed, but I had just talked to you. It took me a while to put it together."

He nodded somberly. "A lot of luck and guesswork, then."

"Right," Aggie agreed. "Mostly I was following the trail Mr. Fisher left, which was pretty clumsy."

"It gets clumsier," McMasters assured her.

Aggie said, "Tell me what happened."

"I believe," said McMasters, "this young man had in mind to set off a chain-reaction explosion using det cord and ammonal to activate the old artillery shells that were buried in the field next door where the site of the original park was supposed to be. Not that easy to do with what he had to work with, but it was my signature from the old days, and it looks like he was trying to hang the gig on me. They used to call me Rocketman, you know, because nobody could put together a fireworks show like me. To tell the truth, I've got to admire the kid for even trying."

Aggie looked at her watch. "The bomb threat said eighty-two minutes. That's almost up."

"Don't worry, Miss Chief, that was all part of the show. First place, he doesn't have the stones to set off a bomb where people might get hurt, especially people he knows. Second place, I stopped him before he could set the charges. When you all started emptying out the park, I figured this was the day it was all going down and got back here to find him laying out the det cord. He was trying to cover it up with his hands so

I wouldn't find it. Would've gone a lot faster with a shovel."

Aggie looked at Fisher. "Is he telling the truth?" she demanded. "Is there a bomb in Mercury Park?"

He shook his head desperately, making muffled sounds behind the tape that covered his mouth.

Aggie looked at McMasters impatiently. "I need to talk to him. Take the tape off his mouth. And put away the shotgun. Please," she added. "I've got it from here."

He shook his head. "No, ma'am," he replied in an easy, laconic drawl. "That's not gonna happen. Not yet."

Aggie took a stride forward and put her hand on the gate. He lifted the shotgun and pointed it at her. "Don't do that," he advised. His tone had hardened, and for the first time Aggie caught a glimpse of the man he once had been. "If you know anything about me at all, you know I won't have a problem using this thing."

Aggie raised a staying hand and stood still. "Okay," she said. Backup was on the way. Grady couldn't be more than five minutes out. All she had to do was keep everyone calm until help got here. "Okay, I'm staying on this side of the fence. But help me to understand what's happening. And please don't point the shotgun at me. So far, you've got a pretty good case for self-defense under Florida's Stand Your Ground law. Threatening a police officer takes that off the table."

He seemed amused by that. "Ah, Miss Chief, you've got to know I'm never going see the inside of a courtroom." Nonetheless, he lowered the shotgun to rest across his knees again.

"You have amnesty for your old crimes," Aggie pointed out. "But any crimes you commit here on Dogleg Island you will be charged with. That's how it works."

He gave a sad shake of his head. "There are some crimes amnesty doesn't cover," he said. He looked at Aaron Fisher. "Isn't that right, kid?"

Fisher, breathing hard through flared nostrils, looked back at him, contempt and fury fighting through the fear in his eyes.

McMasters looked back at Aggie. "I didn't know Tulip was pregnant," he said, "not until after she was sentenced. Hell, I didn't even know Karen Little was her real name, and Cappy—that was the father, Aaron's father... I don't know if he ever even knew he had a kid. I heard he was shanked in the shower about ten years in. I kept up with them. I wasn't supposed to, but I had to, you know? I don't have internet out here, but every time I went across the bridge, I'd use the computers at the library over there. After a while, I got one of those smart phones, which made it a lot easier. And when I heard about the boy, Tulip's boy, well... I guess I always knew this day was coming."

Aggie glanced down at Flash. His ears were rotated slightly as he listened for Grady's approach, but his eyes were fixed on McMasters, and the hands that rested so readily on the shotgun.

She said, "You couldn't have known he'd found you. What made you think Aaron was coming here?"

"The podcast," McMasters replied simply. "The

damn fool told the world he'd located the secret hideout of Richard Dunhill on one of Florida's Gulf Coast barrier islands. He didn't broadcast his whole interview with Tulip, but I figured that's where it came from. I had this magazine, and I used to talk about Dogleg Island while we were planning our last job..." He gave a slow, sad shake of his head. "The Mercury Oil Building job. I know it's going to sound crazy. Probably is. But I kind of felt a responsibility to this island, after what Mercury Oil did. Not that we could have stopped it, even if the job had gone off like we planned. I knew that, even back then. No matter how many buildings we blew up, oil was going to keep on leaking into the Gulf. Beaches were going to keep on disappearing. Fish were going to keep on dying. Still, I kept thinking that one last job might have made some kind of difference, you know? And I felt bad. Felt bad about a lot of things. So I settled here, tried to live a good life, add a little beauty here and there where I could." He shrugged. "Not enough, I know. Not nearly enough."

Aggie glanced at Aaron. "It would be nice to hear some of this from him. Lives are at stake, Mr. McMasters. If you're wrong about the bomb..."

He smiled. "Check your watch, Miss Chief. Time's up. If a bomb had been found, your radio and your phone would be lighting up like Christmas Eve. No, he was just trying to get all the law enforcement in the county on the other side of the island so he could work his magic here."

Aggie said, still looking at Fisher, "The det cord?"

McMasters made a small sound that might have been a chuckle. "Harmless, unless it's triggered by a catalyst. It just seemed like a poetic way to keep him constrained, all things considered. Wouldn't you agree?"

Aggie was counting in her head. How far away could Grady be? Was he on the property now, hiding behind a corner of the house or an outbuilding, listening to every word, choosing his moment? She glanced at Flash. She didn't think so.

She said, "How did you know his plan? And if you did, why didn't you call the police? A lot of people were put in danger by that bomb threat today. If you knew what was going to happen, you should have reported it."

He gave a small chuckle. "Seriously, Miss Chief? Like I really need police in my life?" He shook his head briefly. "I followed him," he said, "from the minute he arrived on the island. I've still got some skills left from the old days. The only problem is..." One corner of his mouth turned down wryly, "maybe they're not quite as sharp as they used to be. This morning at the dock, I saw this shady-looking dude—Keagan, I think his name was—give Fisher a roll of det cord and a shovel. The shovel made no sense to me, but the det cord... well, I knew whatever he was going to use it for couldn't be good. Anyhow, Fisher put the cord in the back of his truck, but the shovel was kind of leaning up against the pickup and it fell to the ground when he drove off. Isn't that a hell of a thing? Something that stupid, right?"

He gave a single mournful shake of his head, and then picked up the story. "Anyhow, Keagan picked up the shovel and started to run after Fisher and that's when he saw me there in the shadows next to one of the boats, watching. He came at me, swinging that shovel, and I don't mind telling you it was touch and go there for a minute. But I guess if you've spent the past fifty years working with your hands and your muscles you've still got an edge over a twenty-five-year-old addict. I twisted the shovel out of his hands and swung back. I didn't mean to kill him," he added, somewhat flatly. "Didn't know he was going to go into the water. But I don't guess the world is any the worse off now that he's gone."

Aggie said carefully, "I'm not going to disagree with you there. But a good lawyer could make a case for accidental homicide which might be viewed as an attempt to aid in the apprehension of a felon. You might not even do time." Aggie was making this up as she went, and she felt no shame in it. Where was Grady?

His expression was not so much disbelieving as disinterested. "I thought about leaving the shovel there at the scene, but then I figured if you found it in Fisher's truck, that might slow him down some." He smiled dryly. "It was no problem getting into the campground where they were staying, but in the dark I couldn't tell which truck was Fisher's. Like I said, seventy-two years old. Slowing down a little." He shrugged. "So I hid it in the first truck I found and hoped for the best."

"Fisher is not going to get away with this," Aggie assured him. "He broke into two public buildings and stole records and caused grievous harm to an elderly citizen, in addition to what he's done here. Let me take him into custody. I can promise you justice will be served."

McMasters shook his head slowly. "I don't mean to doubt your word, ma'am, but that doesn't seem likely." The shadows that gathered in his eyes were almost unbearably sad. "I built a good life here, Chief," he said. "Some might say better than I deserve. But I worked hard to live up to the person I'd decided to become, and now it's over. No matter what happens, I'll never be McMasters the gardener again. People won't come to me to buy their lilies or ask me to design their front yards or donate plants to the community center. I can't be that person anymore. I can only be Richard Dunhill the terrorist for the rest of my life. Which, the way I see it—and I guess this is the good news—won't be very long."

"It doesn't have to be that way," Aggie said. "You can't know the future, and you're not the same person you were in your twenties. You can still have a good life."

He smiled faintly. "Nah, Miss Chief. I appreciate the effort but, like the fella says, you've gotta know when to fold 'em."

Aggie said, "Let Fisher go, Mr. McMasters. You know you're going to have to do it sooner or later. Turn him over to me, and let's all work this out down at the police station."

McMasters did not move. "Well, now," he replied regretfully, "that's where we have a problem. A couple of them, in fact. The first is, he's set up a trip wire somewhere and I haven't found it yet. I figured sitting here in the sun with his mouth taped shut for a while might give him a chance to think over exactly what to say the next time I ask him where it is. The second is, you know those old artillery shells he was trying to set off in the field? They're not there anymore. Truth is, I've been collecting them over the years, using them as a kind of perimeter barrier to protect my property just in case something like this ever happened."

Aggie stared at him. "Do you mean—like a mine field?"

"That's right," he replied easily. "I never had any reason to activate the field before, but any kind of explosion is bound to trigger a sympathetic reaction and we're all going to be in a world of hurt. So the first thing we've got to do is find the live charge this idiot set and deactivate it. And so far, he hasn't been sufficiently motivated to tell me where it is."

Aggie pressed the button on her collar radio. "Grady," she said sharply. "Stop moving. The ground is mined. Stay where you are and call in the bomb squad. Do you copy?"

There was no reply.

Frantically, Aggie pushed the button again. "Grady! Do you copy?"

McMasters looked mildly concerned. "There are a couple of dead zones out here," he said. "If he's in one of them, he won't hear you."

"Grady!" she shouted into the radio now. "Grady, acknowledge!"

Nothing.

Aggie changed the channel on her radio. "This is Chief Malone, Dogleg Island Police, requesting emergency response from the bomb squad at 16 Orchid Lane. We have a hostage situation, and the perimeter is mined with live artillery shells. Repeat, the perimeter is mined. Approach with caution."

Even before she finished speaking, Aggie was dialing Grady's number. She let it ring four times and disconnected. If he was able, he would have answered on the first ring. She sent a text as quickly as she could. *Perimeter is mined! Trip wire in place. Don't move!*

She shoved the phone in her pocket and grasped the gate latch. McMasters got to his feet and swung the shotgun on her. Aggie pushed through the gate with such force that he had no chance to prepare for what she was about to do. She wrested the weapon from him in a single move and he staggered back, watching as she ejected the cartridges on the ground. Aggie threw the shotgun over the fence and pivoted to Fisher, reaching him in what felt like a single stride. Flash crouched between Aggie and McMasters, holding the man with his stare.

Aggie ripped the tape off Fisher's mouth. "Where is it?" she demanded hoarsely. "Where is the trip wire?"

Fisher struggled against his bonds and the flimsy lawn chair threatened to tip over. "He deserves to die!" Fisher shouted back. "He deserves to die the same way all those people he killed did!"

"*Where is it?*" Aggie grabbed his ponytail and jerked his head back, banging it hard against the aluminum frame of the chair. "Talk to me, damn it!"

Fisher gasped with pain as she tightened her grip on his hair, pulling his head farther back. The front legs of the chair left the ground. "He was the ringleader," Fisher said through tightly clenched teeth. "Everything that happened, it was all on him. And he walked away! I was a prison baby, farmed out to foster care. My parents were sent away to rot in separate prisons. It took me almost forty years to find out who they even were! So yeah, let him spend a little time wondering if his next step is going to be his last. And if there's any justice in this world, it will be!"

Aggie released his hair abruptly and stepped back, drawing her firearm. She bent down to look at Fisher, eye level, holding the gun pointed steadily two inches away from the bridge of his nose. His eyes went dark with alarm, and he tried to shrink back but was prevented by his restraints.

"Listen to me," Aggie said quietly. "My husband is out there, the father of my child, and I can promise you that if I hear an explosion, I am going to pull this trigger because at that point I will have nothing left to lose. Do you understand me?"

He nodded stiffly, shock joining the terror in his eyes now that he knew the threat was imminent and that it involved someone other than McMasters.

Aggie said, "Did you set a trip wire attached to an explosive?"

He nodded, once.

"Where is it?"

"I…" His Adam's apple convulsed as he swallowed. "It's … there were a lot of charges. That's the only one I had time to connect. I can't remember."

Aggie jammed the barrel of the pistol into the bridge of his nose. His eyes squeezed shut. "Remember!" she shouted.

"Okay!" he gasped. Sweat trickled down his face. "I can't… I can't tell you. I have to show you."

Aggie straightened up and swung back to McMasters. "Untie him," she commanded.

He shook his head slowly. "Miss Chief," he said, "he's lying. He's not going to show you where it is, even if he does remember."

"I'll know it when I see it," Fisher assured Aggie frantically. "I'm not lying!"

"Untie him!" Aggie repeated to McMasters, raising her gun toward him to emphasize the command.

McMasters held both hands out to his sides, palms down, in a placating gesture.

"Wire cutters are in my pocket," he said.

She gave a short nod.

Aggie held her breath when McMasters cut the det cord, and so, she thought, did Fisher. But he had told the truth. It wasn't live. McMasters cut the gardening wire that bound Fisher's feet, and then his hands. Fisher staggered upright, rubbing his wrists. Aggie shot a quick glance at McMasters. "Can you disarm this thing if he finds it?"

He gave a single decisive nod. "I can."

"Then let's go." She gestured sharply with her

weapon to Fisher. "Move," she said.

He swiped a forearm across his forehead. His hand was shaking. "It's… it was at the back. Near a path, by the greenhouse."

Aggie waved McMasters into position behind him. "Go."

They moved forward. Aggie followed six steps behind the two men, her gun at the ready, Flash at her side.

There was another gate at the corner of the house leading to an open area where the hoop houses and potting sheds were. Aggie scanned the area with her eyes. No sign of Grady.

McMasters leaned across Fisher to unlatch the gate. Fisher shoved him hard, and he stumbled backwards. Fisher plunged through the gate at a run, slamming it back so that it bounced against its supports and caught the latch again. Aggie shouted, "Stop!" She fumbled with the latch. "Stop or I'll shoot!"

Fisher kept running.

Flash leapt over the gate in hot pursuit. Aggie had a clear shot at Fisher, and she called, "Flash, get down!"

Flash dropped to the ground. Aggie sited her target, aiming for the center of his back.

McMasters caught her arm. "Don't!" he gasped. "Chain reaction. If your bullet hits the wrong thing…"

But he never got a chance to finish the warning, because in that moment a fireball erupted in front of them, and the percussive force knocked them both off their feet.

CHAPTER TWENTY-FIVE

Flash put his paws on Aggie's shoulders, nudging her face with his nose. Aggie closed her fingers around his fur, coughing, dazed. The heat from the fire was like a sunburn on her face and cinders rained down on her hair. "Ryan," she gasped.

She managed to get onto her hands and knees, and she felt McMasters close his hand around her arms, helping her to her feet. "Ryan!" she screamed. She tried to run but the older man held her back with a surprisingly strong grip. "*Ryan!*"

"Stay back, Chief," McMasters said, shouting to be heard over the roar of the flames. His face was streaked with soot and dirt, his eyes squinting in the smoke. "Fisher must've have tripped the wire. There'll be more blasts!"

"Let me go! Let me go, you fool!" She wrestled her arm away, but even as she shouted another explosion shook the ground on which she stood. Flames shot over the roof of the cottage and smoke painted the bright sky purple. Her eyes watered and she gagged on the acrid taste of the smoke, wiping her eyes with her sleeve.

McMasters shouted, "Stay here!" And he ran toward the fire, head down, arm raised to shield his eyes.

Aggie dropped to the ground, sweeping the sand for her gun. She found it and holstered it. But before she could go after McMasters, another blast drove her to her knees, followed almost immediately by another. The world around her was on fire.

Flash was torn. His job was to take care of Aggie, but Grady was in trouble and Aggie couldn't help him. The air was thick with the taste of smoke and ashes, melting plastic and crackling pine wood. It was hard to breathe. One of the hoop houses crumpled like an old lady in bad shoes and sank to the ground. Flames wrapped the branches of a tall pine tree, making it look like a single birthday candle swaying in the wind. Grady and Aggie. Aggie and Grady. There couldn't be one without the other. Flash had no choice. He ran toward the fire.

Aggie cried, "Flash!"

But if Flash looked back, Aggie couldn't see him through the smoke.

Aggie staggered to her feet, coughing into her elbow as she tried to shield her face from the smoke. The roof of the cottage was on fire, shingles popping like corn in a kettle. The wind rushed the flames through the undergrowth, fanning them up the trunks of trees. A large pane in the greenhouse twenty yards away cracked with a sound like a gunshot. Sparks sailed across the sand drive, igniting the dry pine straw that formed the forest floor in the woods opposite. Waves of fire surged across the ground, spewing a fog of smoke so thick Aggie could no longer see her feet.

"Flash!" she cried again. But her voice was choked and hoarse and didn't carry very far. "*Ryan!*"

And that was when she heard the barking.

Aggie stumbled toward the sound. The field in back of the house that once had been the site of Mercury Park rippled with a dozen separate fires. The sky rained red-hot cinders and flaming debris and the smoke blotted out the sun. Aggie followed the sound of muffled barking, dodging burning timbers that were the remains of outbuildings, breathing shallowly through the crook of her arm and wiping her streaming eyes. "Flash!" She tried to shout the word, but the effort set off a fit of coughing and stole her voice.

Suddenly Flash was there, bursting through the smoke as though it was a physical barrier. He barked once, then spun back the way he had come. Aggie ran after him.

She had only gone a few hundred steps when she saw them both, shadows in the fog: Grady limping toward her, Flash running back and forth between them. Aggie threw herself at her husband, wrapping him in her arms, whispering, "Oh my God, oh my God."

He hugged her back even as he staggered with the force of her embrace. His voice was hoarse as he said, "Babe, am I glad to see you."

She took his face in her hands. It was streaked with sweat and soot, and blood trickled from a wound on his forehead. She wiped the blood away with her fingers, searching anxiously for other injuries. "What happened?"

"Trapped by part of a shed when it went up," he managed between coughs. "McMasters pulled me out. But the smoke… not sure I would have found you without Flash."

Aggie dropped briefly to her knees and hugged Flash hard. He grinned back at her and licked a smoky tear from her face.

Grady looked at her gravely as she stood again. "Babe, Fisher didn't make it. He must have hit a wire. That was the first blast."

She nodded, slipping her arm around his waist. "Can you walk? Lean on me."

"Turned my ankle is all," he said. His weight was unsteady against her as they made their way back toward the flaming house. "Need to get out of here. This thing is spreading fast."

Aggie pushed the button on her radio again. "This is Chief Malone. We need fire and rescue at this location. Multiple structure involvement, brush fires igniting. And an ambulance. One injury, one deceased." Dispatch acknowledged, and she clicked off.

"Nothing to stop the fire on this side of the island,"

Grady said hoarsely, "we're going to have to start an evacuation."

They ducked to avoid a piece of flaming debris from the house and moved as quickly as possible toward the safety of Aggie's vehicle. Flash sailed over the fence and waited for them in front of the SUV. The sound of sirens was growing close. Help was on the way.

Aggie paused as they reached the gate, looking back. "Where is Mr. McMasters?"

Grady turned, too. Both of them called. They waited as long as they could. But he was gone.

CHAPTER TWENTY-SIX

The fire raged for two and a half days, burning several hundred acres and doing extensive damage to the lush wilderness that was the wildlife refuge. Two homes were damaged, both unoccupied, but no lives were lost. Aggie and Flash went door-to-door while Grady was being stitched up in the ER, trying to get people to safety. The fire moved so fast that the only safe place for many was the beach, and that's where they went.

Deer and possum and racoons and snakes and wild pigs fled their turpentine forest home and flooded the streets and pathways of Dogleg Island. Someone took a cell phone video of Flash herding a group of panicked deer away from the smoke and toward the safety of the beach, and it went viral. The Panama City television station picked it up and played it over and over again. Someone nominated Flash for the Canine

Hero of the Year Award. Flash wasn't sure what that meant, but he was glad none of the deer were hurt. He burned his paws, but the vet fixed him up just fine with some cream and some sporty red bandages, and he hardly even noticed after an hour or two.

The rain came, stopping the fire from spreading to the populated side of the island, leaving a veil of smoke and a graveyard of blackened earth and skeletal trees behind. The streets ran black with soot, and residents spent days scrubbing the oily mess off their windows, but no one complained. They were glad they still had windows to wash.

Mason McMasters, aka Richard Dunhill, was never found. Despite the fire department's most diligent search of every inch of the premises, they located no trace of any victim besides Fisher. Perhaps, if he had survived, he had been relocated by the government once again. Perhaps he had relocated himself. Aggie privately told Grady she did not think they would ever know, but she hoped he had found a way to live out his last days in peace. Despite his crimes, he had lived the life of a good man for almost fifty years. And he had saved her husband's life. That was worth everything.

By Friday, the emergency was mostly over, and Aggie and Flash were back in the office again. Somehow it felt different now. The spooky shadows and remembered cries of terror that had haunted the hallways were no longer perceptible. The light that streamed through the high windows seemed brighter, the buzz of telephones and the clatter of voices were busy and welcoming. The new office was starting to feel like home.

Flash had heard one of the firemen telling Aggie that sometimes it was necessary to burn everything down in order for new things to grow, and that when the forest came back after the fire it would be even stronger and lusher than it had been before. Flash thought that might be true about other things, too. At any rate, that was one of the things he liked to think about while he lay on his red plaid bed in their new office, chewing a bone and resting his paws. Things were different now. A lot was gone. But new things were growing.

While Flash chewed his bone—doing his best not to crunch too loudly—and thought about these things, Aggie sat at her desk, looking at Lucy with an expression of great resolve on her face. She said, "There are a couple of things you need to understand. First of all, this is strictly probationary. Three months, then we'll review."

Lucy, dressed today in crisp blue trousers and a buttoned-up white shirt with her hair in a neat coil atop her head, gave a single sharp nod. "Of course."

"Secondly," Aggie went on, "our personal relationship ends at the door. Here, I'm your boss. I give the orders, you do what I say. Strictly professional."

Lucy replied, "Understood."

So far, Aggie thought she was doing quite well. Get off on the right foot, that was the key. Establish the chain of command clearly and firmly from the beginning so that there could be no possible misunderstanding.

She went on, "Office hours are from 8:00 to 5:00 Monday through Friday but you should be prepared to work overtime on a moment's notice. You need to be here by 7:30 to open the office and take no more than an hour for lunch each day. You never, and I mean *never* leave your desk without turning the phones over to 911. You get Thanksgiving, Christmas, and New Year's Day off, no other holidays. Two weeks' vacation after a year. Questions?"

Lucy gave her a vaguely condescending smile. "I've read the employee handbook, Aggie."

"Chief," Aggie corrected, proud of herself. "While we're at work, you should call me Chief Malone."

"Yes, ma'am," she returned pertly. "Anything else?"

"No." Aggie closed Lucy's personnel file and put it in her out basket. "Finish out the day with Sally Ann, and I'll see you bright and early Monday morning."

Lucy stood. "I'll be here."

When she was gone, Aggie collapsed against the back of her chair, closing her eyes. "She is going to walk all over me," she muttered.

She'd barely gotten the words out when the door opened again. Aggie sat up straight.

"Excuse me, Chief," Lucy said. "Captain Grady is here."

Aggie started to make some humorous remark, but then realized Lucy was playing it straight. Doing her job. "Send him in," she said.

Grady came in with a sack of submarine sandwiches and two milkshakes. He grinned as Lucy closed the door behind him. "How'd it go?"

Aggie replied, more confidently than she felt, "Good, I think. I told her what was expected of her and made sure she knows who's boss. It's going to be fine."

Grady put the milkshakes on her desk and started to unpack the bag. Flash came over to greet him, and Grady gave his ears a quick rub. "Babe, she's going to walk all over you."

Aggie sighed, trying not to look too despondent. "I know. But I didn't have a choice. Today is Sally Ann's last day. And you've got to admit, Lucy was a big help during the fire, not to mention her contribution to the Fisher case. It's going to be fine," she repeated, trying to make herself believe it.

Grady unwrapped Flash's sub—hold the pickles, hold the dressing, hold the bun—and put it in his bowl, then pulled up a chair in front of Aggie's desk. His limp was barely noticeable now and the gash on his forehead was healing nicely beneath the butterfly tape. Nonetheless, Bishop had granted him medical leave for the rest of the week, which Grady had mostly used to help his neighbors deal with the fire.

"Guess who just bought the Shipwreck?" he said, unwrapping his sandwich.

Aggie, who had just taken a bite of her own sandwich, raised her brows in question.

Grady grinned. "Bishop and Dad."

Aggie almost choked on her surprise, and Flash looked up from his turkey and cheese, delighted. The Shipwreck *and* the maritime museum? Both of them, his to visit anytime he wanted? Could it be possible?

Aggie swallowed quickly and took a sip of her milkshake. "You're kidding! They never said a word, not either of them!"

"Well, you know these old guys. They know how to play it close to the vest. And," he added, breaking open a bag of chips, "I guess at a certain point you start wanting something different. Craving it, even. And neither one of them has ever been the kind to shy away from a risk."

Aggie helped herself to a potato chip, smiling as she thought about it. "Well, I think it's fabulous. You couldn't ask for a better match."

"Hell, I knew Bishop wouldn't retire, not really. And this is Dad's dream job—sitting around all day telling fish tales and selling bait. They talked Mr. Obadiah into staying the rest of the year, but the two of them will take over after Bishop retires in January."

Aggie thought about where they would be in January: the family all together again, Bishop and Salty taking over an island institution, Lorraine and Lil and herself shopping for baby clothes… of course she'd be as big as a house by then, but that was a good thing too. In fact, just thinking about it broadened her smile.

She said, "Speaking of January, did you file for the election yet?"

She saw the light go out of his eyes with the mention of the election, although he tried to hide it. "Not yet," he admitted. "I have until 5:00, and I can do it online."

Aggie bit into another chip, watching him

thoughtfully. "Bishop said you never do anything I don't want you to."

His brows drew together in annoyance. "That's total BS. I do lots of things you don't want me to."

"Like what?"

"Like have nachos for lunch. And wash towels without fabric softener. And wear my socks two days in a row."

"You would never do that."

"I might if I wanted to."

Aggie said, "I don't want you to run for sheriff."

He paused in the act of taking a bite from his sub, staring at her. "What?"

"I don't think it's a good move for you," she said. "For us. For the family."

He put his sandwich down, confusion clouding his gaze. "But I thought you were all for it. The money, the hours, the benefits..."

She shook her head. "You were right. No job security. A four-year stint is no way for a family man to live. You hate paperwork and, babe, no offense, but you suck at it. You'd hate being stuck behind a desk. And you hate politics. In fact, you've hated the whole idea since I brought it up."

He frowned. "Not entirely. Well," he admitted, "maybe mostly. But I've got to tell you, hon, I can't see myself working for either one of those jerks who are running now. No matter who wins, I've been his boss at one time or another and hurt a few feelings along the way. I don't think either one would go out of his way to make me comfortable if he was in charge. So either way, I'm probably out of a job come January."

Aggie sipped her milkshake. "Not," she said, "if you come to work for me."

He started to laugh, then stopped himself. "Wait. You're serious."

"I have an opening to fill," she replied practically, "and you're looking for a job. I'm not going to find anyone more qualified than you, or..." she smiled, "anyone I'd rather work with."

He still seemed amused. "Well, I appreciate that but, babe, come on. We can't live on what you can afford to pay me. We've got a baby coming."

"Actually," she countered, "you might be the only lawman I know who *can* afford to live on a Dogleg Island PD salary. Your house is paid for, your wife has a good job, you'd have no commuting expenses. Besides," she added, "it's part time. You'd be rotating hours with Mo, which would give you plenty of time to be at home with baby Lori when you need to. Or," she added, taking a bite of her sandwich, "pick up another job if you wanted to. Maybe even start a business, like Salty and Bishop."

"Lori," he said, and smiled. "I like it." But she could see the wheels turning behind his eyes. He was thinking about her proposal.

Aggie chewed and swallowed, her expression innocent. "Of course, if you think you'd have a problem taking orders from your wife..."

He smothered a guffaw. "Like that would be something new."

Aggie put down her sandwich, her eyes serious

now. "You know how hard it's been for me to think about replacing Sam," she said. "It's not because he was such a great officer—he was, or he would have been, but he'd barely started here and the truth is, he wasn't irreplaceable. It's just that, you know, sticking some pimply-faced rookie in the job seemed disrespectful. Like I was dishonoring his memory. And I think I would have always resented whoever was in the job because of that."

Grady reached across the desk and squeezed her fingers, his expression softened with compassion. "I know, honey."

"But." She squared her shoulders. "I need help. I've got a baby coming and an island to take care of and I can't do it by myself. You are not a compromise, Ryan Grady. You are a trophy. And," she added, picking up her sandwich again, "it would be nice to have someone around the office who's not going to go into shock if I accidentally flash a boob while nursing the baby."

"Well," he agreed, "there's that." He chuckled and picked up his own sandwich. "You, me, Lucy... the entire Dogleg Island Police Department run by Gradys. Talk about your nepotism."

"Also," she pointed out, "I could use someone to run interference between me and Lucy if she's going to stay. So what do you say? Do you accept?"

He was silent while he took another bite of his sandwich and chewed. "Let me think about it," he said.

Flash licked his bowl clean and stretched out in his dog bed, utterly content. There was a time, after all, for standing watch at the window, and a time for closing your eyes and thinking about things. What he was thinking about was how things hardly ever turned out the way you expected, and how most of the time that was a good thing. How change could be scary when you were in the middle of it, but in the end green things would start to grow again. He thought about shrimp floating in tanks at the Shipwreck, and about the bones of whales at the maritime museum and how sometimes the things you hardly even dared to hope for could be yours.

Behind the lids of his closed eyes, he could see things growing, bigger and better than ever before.

BOOKS BY
DONNA BALL

The Dogleg Island Mystery Series

FLASH
Dogleg Island Mystery #1

Almost two years ago the sleepy little community of Dogleg Island was the scene of one of the most brutal crimes in Florida history. The only eye witnesses were Flash, a border collie puppy, and a police officer. Now the trial of the century is about to begin. The defendant, accused of slaughtering his parents in their beach home, maintains his innocence. The top witnesses for the prosecution are convinced he is lying. But only Flash knows the truth. And with another murder to solve and a monster storm on the way, the truth may come to late... for all of them.

THE SOUND OF RUNNING HORSES
Dogleg Island Mystery #2
A family outing takes a dark turn when Flash, Aggie and Grady discover a body on deserted Wild Horse

Island, and the evidence appears to point to someone they know—and trust.

FLASH OF BRILLIANCE
Dogleg Island Mystery #3
Aggie, Flash and Grady look forward to their first Christmas as a family until a homicide hit-and-run exposes a crime syndicate, and dark shadows from the past return to haunt their future.

PIECES OF EIGHT
Dogleg Island Mystery #4
A deadly explosion at an archeological dig on Dogleg Island plunges police chief Aggie Malone and her canine partner Flash into a dark mystery from the past, while on the other side of the bridge, Deputy Sheriff Ryan Grady stumbles onto the site of a mass murder. As the investigation unfolds, Aggie and Grady see that the two cases are related, but only Flash knows how...and by whom.

FLASH IN THE DARK
Dogleg Island Mystery #5
Flash discovers an abandoned child on the beach, and the subsequent attempt to identify her leads to a secret organization with a plan for revenge that has been decades in the making. Unless Aggie, Grady and Flash can stop it they risk losing everything the love... even Dogleg Island itself.

THE GOOD SHEPHERD: A Dogleg Island Short Novella

A missing infant, a holiday pageant, and a priest determined to do the right thing no matter what the cost all come together to present Dogleg Island police chief Aggie Malone and her canine assistant Flash with one of their most unusual cases yet. When a routine call escalates into a kidnapping on the eve of the annual Dogleg Island Police Department holiday open house, Flash and Aggie are held hostage by a desperate man whose only chance for redemption may be the grace of the holiday season.

Also Available in *DECK THE HALLS: A HOLIDAY MYSTERY ANTHOLOGY*

The Raine Stockton Dog Mystery Series
                    Books in Order

SMOKY MOUNTAIN TRACKS
A child has been kidnapped and abandoned in the mountain wilderness. Her only hope is Raine Stockton and her young, untried tracking dog Cisco...

RAPID FIRE
Raine and Cisco are brought in by the FBI to track a terrorist ...a terrorist who just happens to be Raine's old boyfriend.

GUN SHY
Raine rescues a traumatized service dog, and soon begins to suspect he is the only witness to a murder.

BONE YARD
Cisco digs up human remains in Raine's back yard, and mayhem ensues. Could this be evidence of a serial

killer, a long-unsolved mass murder, or something even more sinister... and closer to home?

SILENT NIGHT
It's Christmastime in Hansonville, N.C., and Raine and Cisco are on the trail of a missing teenager. But when a newborn is abandoned in the manger of the town's living nativity and Raine walks in on what appears to be the scene of a murder, the holidays take a very dark turn for everyone concerned.

THE DEAD SEASON
Raine and Cisco take a job leading a wilderness hike for troubled teenagers, and soon find themselves trapped on a mountainside in a blizzard... with a killer.

ALL THAT GLITTERS: A Holiday Short Story e book
Raine looks back on how she and Cisco met and solved their first crime in this Christmas Cozy short story. Sold separately as an e-book or bundled with the print edition of HIGH IN TRIAL.

HIGH IN TRIAL
A carefree weekend turns deadly when Raine and Cisco travel to the South Carolina low country for an agility competition.

DOUBLE DOG DARE
A luxury Caribbean vacation sounds like just the ticket for over-worked, over-stressed Raine Stockton and her happy go lucky canine companion Cisco. But even in paradise trouble finds them, and when someone she loves is threatened Raine must use every resource at her command to track down a killer before it's too late.

HOME OF THE BRAVE

There's a new dog in town, and Raine and Cisco find themselves unexpectedly upstaged by a flashy K-9 addition to the sheriff's department. But when things go terribly wrong at a mountain camp for kids and dogs over the Fourth of July weekend, Raine and Cisco need all the help they can get to save themselves, and those they love.

DOG DAYS

Raine takes in a lost English Cream Golden Retriever, and the search for her owner leads Raine and Cisco into the hands of a killer. Readers will enjoy a treasure hunt for the titles of all ten of the Raine Stockton Dog Mysteries hidden in this special tenth anniversary release!

LAND OF THE FREE

On a routine search and rescue mission Raine Stockton and her golden retriever Cisco stumble onto something they were never meant to find, and are plunged into a nightmare of murder, corruption and intrigue as figures from her past re-emerge to threaten everything Raine holds dear.

DEADFALL

Hollywood comes to Hanover County, and Raine and Cisco get caught up in the drama when a series of mishaps on the set lead to murder.

THE DEVIL'S DEAL

Raine takes temporary custody of what may well be the most valuable dog in the world, but when lives are at stake she is forced to make an unthinkable choice.

MURDER CREEK

Raine and Cisco rescue a dog who is locked in a hot car in a remote Smoky Mountain park... and subsequently discover the owner of that car drowned in the creek only a few dozen yards away. Was it an accident, or was it murder?

ANGELS IN THE SNOW: A Raine Stockton Short Novella

While preparing for the annual Dog Daze Christmas party, Raine leaves on a secret Christmas errand and becomes trapped in a blizzard. Injured and alone, with a desperate criminal on the loose, a surprising canine hero comes to her rescue. But is it all a product of her imagination, or a genuine Christmas miracle?

Also available in in DECK THE HALLS: A HOLIDAY MYSTERY ANTHOLOGY

THE JUDGES DAUGHTER

In this pivotal fifteenth book in the ground-breaking Raine Stockton Dog Mystery Series, the death of an old friend leaves Raine Stockton with an unwanted inheritance, an old wound reopened, and the most challenging mystery of her life.

The Blood River Mystery Series

Don't miss this exciting first installment

UNFIXABLE: A Buck Lawson Mystery

Former sheriff Buck Lawson leaves the mountains of North Carolina to take a job as police chief of the small

South Georgia town of Mercy, and soon finds himself in over his head. For one thing, his predecessor has been murdered...

UNSTOPPABLE:
With the Fourth of July coming up and the Mercy police force already stretched to the limit, police chief Buck Lawson investigates a fraud complaint that leads him to a missing newborn and a terrified, runaway mother. At the same time, the skeletal remains of two young boys are discovered on the property of a prominent citizen. As the investigation unfolds, Buck begins to suspect that the key to both his cases may lie buried with crimes of the past.

WELCOME TO BETHLEHEM: A Buck Lawson Short Novella

Police chief Buck Lawson wants his first Christmas in his new hometown of Mercy, Georgia, to be a memorable one, both for his family and the police officers under his command. But while preparing to host the traditional police department Christmas party, Buck's home is burglarized by a Middle Eastern man who may be connected to far more violent crimes. As the investigation unfolds and unsettling connections to the past come to light, Buck fears this Christmas will be memorable for all the wrong reasons.

Also Available in the Holiday Anthology ***DECK THE***

HALLS

Also by Donna Ball

The Ladybug Farm series:

A Year on Ladybug Farm
At Home on Ladyug Farm
Love Letters from Ladybug Farm
Christmas on Ladybug Farm
Vintage Ladybug Farm
A Wedding on Ladybug Farm

The Hummingbird House
Christmas At the Humingbird House
The Hummingbird House Presents

ABOUT THE AUTHOR

Donna Ball

Donna Ball is the author of over 100 books under a variety of pseudonyms. Though she has been published in virtually every genre, she is best known for her work in women's fiction, mystery, and suspense. Her novels have been translated into multiple languages  around the world. Her most popular series are the award-winning Raine Stockton Dog Mystery series, the Dogleg Island Mystery series,The Blood River Series, and the Ladybug Farm series. All are available now in paperback, audio and digital downloads for your e-reader.

Donna lives in the heart of the Blue Ridge Divide in a remodeled Victorian-era barn. She spends her spare time hiking, painting, and enjoying her three show-stopping canines.

Made in the USA
Monee, IL
06 December 2023

48309997R00150